I0733458

*want me*


M. MALONE

Want Me by M. Malone

Published by CrushStar Romance

An Imprint of CrushStar Multimedia LLC

440 N. Barranca Ave #9016

Covina, CA 91723

www.MMaloneBooks.com



For permissions contact: CrushStar Multimedia LLC

ISBN 9781938789700 (print) | ISBN 9781938789694 (ebook)

Cover Design © CrushStar Multimedia LLC

Printed in United States of America

First Edition

# contents

*want me*

# *one*

ANYA

I ALWAYS THOUGHT that I'd leave this earth in dramatic fashion.

How would I go, I'd wonder?

Fall to my death off a cliff while hiking?

Drown while white water rafting?

Or something more mundane. Such as a heart attack after spending years eating ice cream and cookies instead of dinner.

But it turns out my time to leave this mortal coil is right here. Right now. Cause of death?

Acute mortification after choking in front of one of the sexiest men I've ever seen.

As my life flashes before my eyes, I'm not inundated with images of all the things I never got to do or with regrets about the past. There's only one thought that's as loud as a bullhorn.

*Am I seriously being taken out by a wedding cupcake?*

## ANYA

*a few months ago...*

"WELL, look who it is. My angel."

The voice pulls me out of my daydreams and I look up to see the smiling face of my parents' doorman. George has worked here for almost as long as I can remember and he always has a smile and a kind word for everyone he meets.

He and his wife, Paula, treat me like one of their own kids and I know she calls to check on my parents a few times a month.

"Hmm, I have no idea what you mean," I tease.

I take my sunglasses off and slide them in my bag. Despite it only being June, the sun glares down from overhead blanketing the nation's capital in heat. DC doesn't wear heat well like California or Florida. Instead it just feels like a sweaty armpit. As much as I love the summer, I'll be grateful when it's over. Some days it feels as if I'll melt right into the pavement.

George tips his head and raises one bushy eyebrow. "I know you're the one sending us the money. You're the only one I told about our financial problems."

"It sounds like you have a secret admirer." It's a struggle not to smile. He won't need much inducement to send the money back if he thinks it's coming from me. He's a proud man and won't accept help if he knew the source.

Which was the reason I'd paid part of his hospital bill anonymously in the first place.

"Anyway, I'm just popping in to see Mom and Dad on my lunch break. She called this morning and said he's having a good day. I'll see you when I come back down. Maybe if Paula is up for it, we can play cards again."

George gives me a shrewd look that says he won't be deterred long by my evasion.

"Say hello to Vik and Marta for me," he says while holding the door for me.

"Will do."

I take the elevator up to the fifth floor and then walk to the first door on the right. My mom opens up as soon as I knock.

"Anya! I'm so glad you could come. He was just asking about you."

My mom's expression is radiant and it's such a relief to see. Too many days her eyes are pinched and her smile strained, the stress of being caretaker to a husband who is often angry and hostile taking a visible toll.

"Hi Pop! What are you doing?"

I throw my bag down on the floor and kneel next to where my father is hunched over at the dining table. The pose brings back memories. When I was little, I would sit in his lap while he read me articles or told me about his research. Not that I understood most of it but the love in his voice needed no explanation. Nothing since has ever made me feel so safe.

"Anya, *lyubov moya*. Come and see what I'm working on."

My heart warms at the way he whispers *my love*, the same way he did when I was a small child. He holds up the paper he's been writing on. It's covered with chemical formulas.

Ah, today he's back in the prime of his career when he was a brilliant young chemist just emigrated from Russia. No wonder my mom said today was a good day. He's always happiest when his mind travels back to before he lost his job at the university and he was still considered a rising star in his field.

"That's great, Pop. Will you tell me about it?"

I lean against the arm of the chair and let the sound of

his voice flow around me. It's amazing how different he can be when the dementia eases its grip on a once brilliant mind. However, it's not long before I can see he's tiring.

"I'll be back in a few days to visit again, Pop. Don't give Mom a hard time." I whisper the last part, hoping it takes root in the back of his mind and stays put even when things get fuzzy again.

There's no room for anger here. It's not his fault that he gets so belligerent on the days when his memory and confusion are worse. The doctors have assured us that personality changes are common in dementia patients. However knowing that it's common doesn't make it any easier for my mother when he's accusing her of poisoning him or screaming for her to leave him alone.

"Maybe you can bring James with you next time." Mom sits on the edge of the chair and pats my father's shoulder fondly.

Wow. She waited a whole twenty minutes before working that into the conversation. A record. A forty-one-year-old divorced workaholic is not exactly what she would have chosen for her only daughter, but he's a man and he's breathing. That's enough to fan the flames of hope in my mother's romantic heart.

"I'm not sure if he can, Mom. He can't really leave in the middle of the day the way I can. He's the boss."

She hums in understanding. "Still, it would be nice to

see him again. I never got to thank him properly for the flowers he sent."

"He sent you flowers?"

This is news to me. Law never said anything about ordering flowers for my mother. Her birthday was last month and he saw me wrapping her gift but he never asked for any details. He can be infuriatingly self-contained that way. I used to think he was completely oblivious since he never asked for details about anything, then I realized that he doesn't talk because he's *listening*.

The man takes it all in for further research later and never forgets a thing.

"Well, that was nice of him."

"Yes, it was. They were the most beautiful peonies. I'm not sure how he knew they were my favorite."

"I must have mentioned it at some point."

"That's the kind of man that will make a thoughtful husband."

"On that note, I have to go."

I lean over and give my father a quick kiss on the cheek. He doesn't even look up, already reabsorbed in his world of formulas and equations. If it weren't for my mother, I think he'd happily stay there forever.

My mom walks me to the door. "You're in quite a rush today."

"I need to get back to the office and finish what I was

working on. I don't want to be held up this evening." Although I usually avoid telling my mother stuff like this because she gets way too excited, I can't help it. I have to tell someone. "Law said he planned something special for tonight. I think he's planning to propose."

My mom places a hand over her heart. "Oh, Anya. You really think so? He's such a good man."

"He is, isn't he?"

I'm usually not so insecure but after the dumpster fire of my last relationship, it's hard to trust my own judgment. But Law is nothing like the men I've known before. Maybe it's because he's older but he knows what he wants and he doesn't play games. I can count on him.

"He is, sweetie. That man loves you. I can tell."

"For once I got it exactly right."

She pulls me into a gentle hug. "Be careful out there, sweetheart."

She says the same thing every time I leave. Back when my father still went to work, she used to say it to him every morning.

"I will. Love you, Mom."

Right before the door closes behind me, I hear her call out, "Call me after! I want to hear every detail!"

I leave with a smile on my face. My mom is one hundred percent going to take over the wedding planning. She'll probably drive me crazy inside of a month but it'll give her something to think about other than doctors, medicine and frustration.

After everything she's been through over the past couple of years, it'll be nice to have something fun to talk about with my mother again.

## LAW

AFTER CLOSING the door to my office, I rest my head against the wood. It's been a long-ass day and it's nowhere near over.

Such is the gift and curse of being the boss.

Not that I don't love it. Owning my own marketing agency has been the culmination of a lifelong dream. I'm not so far removed that I don't remember the early days, eating ramen on the floor of my shitty apartment because I'd rather starve than ask my father for money. I'd worked long hours at my first marketing job, determined to learn everything I could and prove my worth.

I had no way of knowing if it would even be worth it back then but I still showed up every day, burning with the drive to prove myself. To carve out a space in this industry that no one could take away.

Now I'm here and have discovered that the fear of losing it all never goes away. In fact, it's only worse because now I have an audience. My failures have the potential to take out a whole company of faithful employees who are counting on me to lead them.

The phone on my desk rings but I ignore it. After the meeting I just finished, I deserve to be off grid for a bit. New client meetings are usually easy but every once in a while you get one of *those* clients. The ones you just *know* will be more trouble than they're worth. But when you're in business, you have to weigh the potential payday against the trouble.

Big clients don't come around every day and this client alone could cover the agency's payroll for two years.

Minimum.

All I have to do is ignore the little voice in the back of my head. The one screaming *run away*.

Frustrated, I scrub a hand through my hair. The last time I ignored my instincts it turned out to be a mistake. As always, the mental image of Gareth Whittington brings a scowl to my face. On paper, his business seemed sound and although adult entertainment is considered a gray area for a lot of people, I was open to the idea of branching out. It wasn't the nature of his business that gave me pause.

It was *him*.

I didn't want to work for someone who seemed to have

no moral lines. The girls in his raunchy videos were all legal but I got the distinct sense that if they hadn't been, he wouldn't have cared.

That immediately put him in my hell-no category.

Elizabeth convinced me I was being too cautious. It was something she'd teased me about all too often. In the beginning, she'd found it charming.

*Don't be such a grandpa*, she'd say with a smile.

After a few years that smile became a sigh. Then the sigh became a smirk. She stopped calling me grandpa as a joke. No, she had other names for me then.

*Stick in the mud.*

*Boring.*

Then the final name that changed it all.

*Ex-husband.*

It's embarrassing now how much stock I put in her opinion. I worshipped the ground she walked on and she used that knowledge to screw me over and steal most of our clients when she left to start her own agency. It's well known that love makes you vulnerable.

Apparently, it also makes you a dumbass.

Light spills across the surface of the desk when my office door opens suddenly. Startled, I swipe the sheets of paper I was reviewing into a folder and rest my hands on top.

"Sorry, boss. I knocked first but you didn't answer."

Mya Taylor-Hamilton is one of the best marketing agents I have on staff and a newly minted Vice President. Creative and brilliant, she's also a whiz with difficult clients. She's one of the reasons that I don't have to think about Elizabeth anymore. All the accounts that Liz used to handle, Mya took over flawlessly.

"It's fine. What did you need?"

Mya's eyes dart to the folder under my hands. My fingers tighten around the file reflexively.

Not that I was looking at anything I shouldn't have been but thoughts of Elizabeth usually affect me this way. Maybe because my good sense knows she's the last thing I need to think about these days.

"It's time for the staff meeting. I can run it for you if you're too busy."

"No. I'm coming. I need to stretch my legs anyway."

"Great. I'll marshal the troops." With a wink, she shuts the door behind her.

I open the top drawer of my desk to put away the folder and my eyes are drawn to the sage green envelope pushed to the back. Every spring Elizabeth would inevitably buy another sundress in the color or a new pair of shoes. I'd complained about it at the time but after she was gone, I'd missed the soft hues of her clothes hanging in the closet across from mine.

She'd always loved the color.

Enough to use it on her wedding invitation to Gareth.

I slam the drawer.

———

THE STAFF MEETING turns out to be an unexpected bright spot in the middle of my day. For once, every team has positive updates on their projects and we move through our agenda quickly.

Finally something is going right.

I've gotten really lucky over the years, hiring some of the best and savviest agents in the business. Mya's team handles most of our beauty and luxury brands while her husband, Milo, handles men's fashion and sports. Our other team lead, Kevin, handles the technology division. Having the right people at the helm of each division has made my life easier and kept us at the top of the marketing food chain.

We wrap up business quickly and as the meeting breaks up, everyone streams out of the conference room. When I emerge into the hallway, Anya falls into step beside me. She holds out a steaming cup of coffee. I accept it gratefully. Caffeine is on my short list of legal addictions that keep me sane.

"Thank you. What was that for?"

She shrugs. "You looked like you could use it. You had a rough morning, huh?"

For a moment I have no idea what she's talking about. There's no way she could know about the new client yet. I've been careful to keep that info close to the vest. My confusion must be evident because she laughs.

"The staff meeting. I know how much you hate them."

Letting out a relieved sigh, I nod. "That I do but they're a necessary evil. This is exactly what I needed though."

A few more bracing sips of the strong brew and I feel almost normal. It's not technically in Anya's job description to make coffee for anyone, she's our office manager and not an assistant anymore, but she insists on doing it everyday.

Remembering my early attempts to make the coffee remind me of why. For someone who loves it as much as I do, I'm terrible at it. When I make the coffee it tastes more like motor oil.

"Well, I'm hoping that coffee puts you in a better mood so that you'll tell me about this surprise you have for me." She grins widely.

Her cheerful disposition makes it hard to say no to her in general but I have to admit the caffeine boost has definitely put me in a more flexible state of mind.

"I will tell you that it's something you've wanted for a long time."

Her eyes sparkle. "That's all I get?"

"That's all you get." Damn she's cute with her flashing blue eyes and the little dimple that only shows when she's grinning this hard. "Where were you earlier? I was looking for you."

The light in her eyes dims slightly. "My mom called and asked me to come by at lunch. She said Pop was more lucid than usual. "

"I'm glad you went to see him. Maybe you should start doing that more often. Take all the time you need."

She squeezes my arm gratefully. "Maybe I will. You can always call if you need me while I'm out."

"Sure thing."

Even as I say it, I know nothing short of a national emergency would make me call and interrupt her time with her father. His declining condition worries her a lot. She's a woman that loves deeply and it's been breaking her heart knowing there's nothing she can do for him.

"Anyway, I have a few things to finish up so I can get out of here on time. I'll see you later," she whispers before walking down the hall toward her own office.

ANYA

THE REST of the afternoon passes in a blur. I covered the phones so our new receptionist, Sharon, could take her break. Then I hunkered down in my office so I wouldn't be distracted and could leave on time. I arrive at Law's house in the suburbs of Virginia a little before six o'clock.

Law bought this charming little house in the city of Fairfax right after he got divorced. He doesn't talk about that time in his life often but from the things he *has* said, he spent a lot of time doing things *her* way. She wanted the big McMansion in the trendiest zip code so that's what they bought. Only the best furnishings and of course it had to be decorated by some exclusive interior designer.

As I open the front door with my key, I imagine the horror his stuffy ex-wife would feel if she ever got a load of this place. The house is a one-level rancher that reminds me of a sitcom from the eighties. The furniture was clearly all chosen for comfort as opposed to aesthetics since it's all huge and squishy. It looks like a comfortable place to hang out and chill.

It's perfect for us.

Inside the door, there is a small envelope propped up on the entry table. My name is written across the front in Law's signature messy scrawl. I open it slowly, savoring the anticipation.

> *Anya,*
>
> *Tonight I don't want you to worry about anything. Take a relaxing bath and then put on something that makes you feel beautiful. When I get home, I want to take you somewhere special.*
>
> *Law*

Although it's silly, it still bothers me that he never signs notes with anything other than his name. Not that it really matters. It's not like I'm a teenage girl and expect him to write *Love You Always and Forever* with hearts and flowers sketched around his name.

It's just that sometimes it would be nice if he were better at communicating his feelings. He doesn't like to say *I love you* or talk about emotions.

He's stepping outside of his comfort zone to do something romantic. That's the best declaration I could ask for. It's petty to focus on how he signed it instead of the rest of the sweet note. He's had enough of being criticized to last him a lifetime.

Apparently his ex-wife didn't even like that his friends called him *Lawson*. I definitely don't want to call him the same thing she did so I decided on *Law*. Of course, I told him it was because he has a great booty. Which isn't a lie. You could bounce a quarter off the man's ass.

JLo has nothing on him.

In the master bedroom, I shed my work clothes while the bath water runs. My hair is short enough that I don't need to bother with putting it up so as soon as the tub is full, I step into the steaming water. Instantly all my stress floats away as I'm surrounded with a cocoon of heat. I rest my head on the back of the tub and try not to think of anything other than how nice it is to relax and pamper myself.

Who am I kidding? The only thing I can think about is what Law has planned for tonight.

We've been dating off and on for about two years now and we've finally settled into a comfortable rhythm. In the beginning we were both just coming off rough breakups and no-strings attached worked perfectly for us. However, over the past year things have changed. I sleep here more than I sleep at my own apartment. Law keeps all spiders away from me and indulges my obsession with brunch. I keep the fridge stocked since he is a notorious midnight snacker and I also don't mind his frequent golf outings with various friends.

More than that, we can talk about anything. He knows my fascination with different cultures and my yearning to travel. I completely understand his deep desire to build a business legacy to leave behind. We *get* each other and I can't imagine what my life would be like without him in it.

Once my fingers start to look like prunes, I get out of the bath, taking time to smooth on some of the cherry-scented body lotion that Law loves.

I pause in the middle of getting dressed when I hear a door slam in the distance. Suddenly my heart is beating triple time.

The bathroom door opens and Law sticks his head in. "Hey."

"Hey."

We don't say anything else but the way his eyes roam over the black lace bra and panty set I'm wearing says all I need to know.

He groans. "Why did I plan to take you out again?"

"So you could surprise me."

"I've got a surprise for you all right."

I laugh at his shamelessness. "Nothing is stopping me from getting my real surprise."

"Pushy woman," he comments but he's smiling when he says it. "I'll leave you to finish getting ready."

The outfit I chose to wear tonight is a basic white sundress but it clings in all the right places and is unexpectedly comfortable. All I need is to add my favorite gold necklace and some diamond studs and I'm ready for anything.

Since I have no idea where we're going, I don't want to be too dressed up. I catch a glimpse of my face in the mirror as I'm leaving the bathroom and have to pause at how flushed and happy I look. My dark hair is cooperating for once and it makes my blue eyes look brighter.

The excitement that's been on a low burn all day rushes to the fore.

*I'm about to get engaged!*

Law is waiting when I enter the bedroom. He's changed into jeans and a black polo shirt that makes his white hair stand out even more. He is so gorgeous that sometimes it takes my breath away.

"You look beautiful," he says and holds out a hand.

I grab it and let him pull me into the space between his legs. My arms rest on his shoulders as he nuzzles against my neck.

"So do you. But you're wearing jeans so that must mean we're going somewhere casual."

His lips curl against my skin. "Guess all you want. I'm not saying a word."

I follow him out and down the hallway throwing out guesses the whole time.

"Restaurant? Carnival? *Ooh*, art gallery?"

He opens the front door and indicates with a flourish of his arm that I should precede him out the door. The smile on his face tells me he's enjoying keeping this secret.

"Circus? Fundraiser for endangered wildlife? Secret laboratory?"

"All good theories but ...nope."

As Law drives, I take a quick glance around his car. There's nothing on the backseats to provide a clue. Every mile that passes notches my excitement higher and by the time we stop at a local park, I'm ready to burst.

"This is where we're going? This is the surprise?"

He shakes his head. "I never said the surprise was where we were going."

I scramble out of the car after him, not waiting for him to come around and get my door. We meet at the back of the car where Law opens the trunk and then pulls out a picnic basket.

"Come on. Let's find a place to sit."

It's not as hot now that it's after seven o'clock which I'm grateful for. Law finds a shady spot under a tree and then pulls a checkered blanket from the basket on his arm. I take the other side and help him spread it out. Once we sit, he places the basket next to us and starts taking food out.

His basket of wonders is apparently much bigger than it looks because he has silverware, plates and even mini wine glasses inside. In less than five minutes, we have a meal set that looks like it belongs in a magazine.

"I have to say, I am impressed. This is beautiful."

"And you were worried."

"I wasn't worried. Just confused. You know I hate surprises."

He laughs as he pours us some wine. "I do know that. My Type-A Anya. You do like to know everything that is going on."

After a minute, I take a breath and actually start to relax. I should have known Law would plan something like this. We both enjoy things casual and private. He's not the type to plan some showy proposal and I love that about him.

It's just the two of us.

Exactly the way I want it.

"I wanted us to take a moment to relax after how busy things have been. You've been very patient with all the late nights I've been working. I appreciate that a lot."

Even though he means it as a compliment, the praise makes me a little uncomfortable. After all, it's not like I haven't been working a lot as well.

"Of course. I know how important the business is to

you. It's important to me, too. The fact that I get to see you on my breaks and sneak a kiss sometimes makes it even better."

He smiles and takes my hand. "The fact that you get it is just... I don't even know what I would do without you some days. I've been thinking about that a lot lately, how different my life would be if I couldn't look forward to seeing you everyday. I just wanted to find some way to show you how much it means."

He releases my hand and then reaches into his pocket. As my heart trips and falls all the blood rushes to my head.

*Oh my god. This is it!*

He pulls his hand out and hands me an envelope. Confused, I just look at it until he laughs softly.

"Well, open it."

Still stuck between the rush of excitement and confusion about why there's an envelope in my hand instead of a ring box, I just blink for a few moments until Law takes the envelope and opens it.

"It's two tickets to Paris!"

"Paris?" I repeat.

"Yes! I know going to France is on your bucket list and there's a potential client there so I decided, what the hell! Let's make a vacation of it. Just you and me, walking on the Champs-Élysées and eating ... whatever they eat in Paris. It's going to be amazing!"

I laugh weakly, all the anticipation and excitement of a few moments ago fizzling into a puddle of embarrassment and then... guilt. Law is so excited about this amazing trip and I should be too. Going to Paris is something I've wanted for a long time.

"Thank you. This is amazing. I can't believe you planned this." I reach over and pull him into a hug.

After a moment, his arms fold around me. When he tries to pull back, I hold on tighter, not ready to put on a happy face yet. He did this amazing thing for me and all I should be is grateful. Just because I thought it was a proposal and it wasn't doesn't mean anything. People arrive at certain milestones at different points in time. Maybe it's taking Law a little bit longer to feel what I'm feeling and that's okay.

So I'm going to hold on until the dark feeling that came over me when I saw the envelope goes away.

The feeling that I'll be waiting a long time for something that will never come.

## ANYA

*present day...*

PEOPLE ALWAYS SAY that in your final moments your whole life flashes before your eyes. Maybe I'm just not that lucky because all I get is a close up view of a bunch of horrified strangers and the certainty that I haven't done any of the things I wanted to do yet.

*Am I seriously going to die alone?*

Just as I have that cheerful thought, I cough and my airway opens up. Finally. The cool rush of air going down my throat is heaven and I suck in deep breaths until my heart rate slows slightly and the spots in my vision fade.

"Just breathe, *carina.* I've got you." The guy who just saved my life with dramatic use of the Heimlich maneuver stands next to me staring.

Just like all the rest of the people at the table.

My face is still flaming from all the attention and the panic of not being able to breathe a few seconds ago. The source of my mortification sits innocently on my plate, the delicate pink flower crowning the top still intact.

A wedding cupcake.

I didn't even get the dignity of almost being taken out by an entire slice.

"Sorry for the fuss everyone. I'm fine."

Now that I'm no longer in danger of dying, I recognize the handsome man standing next to me as the brother of the groom. I can't remember his name but it was something as ridiculously elegant as the precise fit of his suit.

I wave off his offer of help as I get to my feet, anxious to escape the table. There's an open bar that I've become well-acquainted with over the course of the past hour and I'd much rather cool my mortification over a glass of premium champagne. My heart doesn't slow down until I reach the bar and notice no one I'm familiar with standing there.

Not that it's difficult to find anonymity in this crowd. My friend Casey Michaels just married Andre Lavin, one of the most famous designers on the planet, so the attendees at their wedding range from her mother's nursing friends to minor members of European aristocracy.

I look over the crowd and watch as Andre leads Casey onto the dance floor, her couture gown swirling around her legs like flower petals. It's a Lavin Bridal original and makes her look ethereal, like some kind of otherworldly being. He leans down and whispers something in her ear that brings a tender smile to her lips. The way they look at each other is so intimate it feels voyeuristic to watch.

Envy blooms, quick and nasty, and I turn away. Casey is the sweetest person I know and she deserves every bit of the happiness that has recently come her way.

"Time for the bouquet toss!"

The sudden boom of a voice over the sound system jolts me out of my dazed state. Several women at the surrounding tables groan while others chatter excitedly. I take the opportunity to slip away while everyone else is focused on what's about to happen.

Dodging plant life is really not my thing.

Although, let's be honest. Does anyone actually enjoy the bouquet toss?

From my vast experience being a bridesmaid in all of my friends' weddings, the tradition is the bane of every single girl's life.

You might as well call it "Pin the Tail on the Spinsters!"

Everyone is so focused on the dance floor that no one notices a rogue bridesmaid slipping out a side door and into the hallway. The air is noticeably cooler out here and it feels amazing on my heated skin. Now I just have to find a place to hide out until the bouquet toss is over.

Preferably someplace with alcohol.

My memory of this hotel isn't the best, the Fitz-Harrington isn't exactly in an office manager's price range, but I know there has to be a bar where I can drown my sorrows.

Rich people like to drink too, right?

I take the elevator down to the main lobby and then walk until I see the restaurant up ahead.

For the first time today, I let out a sigh of relief.

The relief is quickly followed by guilt. A close friend has found the love of her life and I'm supposed to be in there supporting her. Instead, I'm hiding out at the bar in another part of the hotel so I don't have to proclaim my perpetual singleness while dodging a flower bomb.

As I sit at the bar and order a glass of wine, I have honestly never felt worse.

Until I turn my head and see the woman sitting two seats over. Her gown is the same peach color as mine but with a slightly different bodice. I was secretly glad the bridesmaid dresses were a little more demure since I don't have the cleavage to carry off a deep v-neck like that.

*"Fucking hell."* Ariana Silva points at me with the same hand holding her drink. "If you're down here…"

I start laughing. "You're the maid of honor!"

She drops her head and bangs it against the polished

mahogany bar top. "We are terrible friends. You know that, right?"

"I'm willing to concede the possibility. To be fair, I almost got killed by a cupcake just now, so I'm probably not making the best decisions."

The bartender sets my drink down in front of me, placing it squarely on the center of a fancy white napkin with a scalloped edge. Resigned to my fate, I hand over my credit card. Starting a tab is the least of my sins at this point.

"Well, at least I don't feel quite as bad now." Ariana raises her glass in my direction with a smirk. "To the last ones standing."

"The last ones."

As I sip my drink, I pray for the alcohol to work quickly. Maybe it can drown out the tears that have been threatening ever since I watched the newlyweds pledge their love to each other.

It's especially awful to be envious of someone as sweet as Casey. Besides it's not like I'm jealous of her life because she doesn't deserve it. She does. And it's not that I want her life exactly. Andre is a handsome man but he's not my type.

Unfortunately I only have a thing for older men with commitment issues.

I thought I was doing a good job of hiding my misery but clearly not since Ari looks over at me with pity.

She motions to the bartender. "I have a feeling we're going to need more drinks."

———

## "SO, WHAT'S YOUR DEAL?"

I can hear myself slurring slightly and it takes me aback.

It's only taken a few drinks to loosen us up. Ariana is a riot and I've always had a good time hanging out with her but usually we're with Casey and our other good friend, Mya. There haven't been that many opportunities for me to hang out with her alone.

"What do you mean?" Ariana seems to be in considerably better shape than I am despite having more drinks.

I pout. Life really isn't fair. The girl looks like a supermodel and apparently also has a steel liver.

My parents are Russian so by all rights, I should be the one who can drink others under the table. Instead I'm barely hanging on. The last thing I need is another embarrassing incident so I signal the bartender and point to my empty water glass.

Maybe if I'd remembered that earlier I wouldn't feel like I'm on the verge of falling off this barstool.

"You're gorgeous. You have the whole Gigi Hadid thing

going on. Why are you drinking at the bar during a wedding? I mean, I know why I'm here."

"Why are you here? Aren't you the one with the hot silver fox boyfriend?"

"The man who wants to keep our relationship a secret? The man who never wants to talk about the future? Is that really a boyfriend or just a man I don't have the willpower to say no to?"

"Ahhh, I think I'm starting to understand. He won't commit. It's a thing. Sounds like we have opposite problems. Your guy won't stay and I can't figure out how to get rid of mine. Maybe we should switch lives."

For some reason this strikes me as really funny and I snort laughing. The bartender places a glass of water in front of me and then leaves just as quickly.

Smart man. I wouldn't want to be involved in this either if it wasn't my sorry life.

I gulp at the water, hoping it'll clear my head. Clearly I'm even more drunk than I thought because most of it goes down the front of my dress. Ari covers her mouth but I can see her shoulders shaking.

"Don't say it. I know I'm a hot mess."

"No, you're just disappointed. I've been there. Men are fun to play with but you can't rely on them. You have to rely on yourself."

"I want to rely on myself. You know, be all independent

woman, hear me roar! But it never seems to work out that way. Tell me how you do it."

She shrugs. "I just do what I want. Men get away with all kinds of bad behavior but women are expected to be perfect. *So stop being perfect.* Just live your life in the moment. See that hot guy over there?"

I glance over my shoulder and follow her line of sight. Then I sigh. The man standing on the other side of the room is gorgeous.

"Wow. Yeah, he is hot."

She winks. "You should ask for his number."

I gape. "What? I can't do that. I h-have a boyfriend."

"Do you? Because I'm pretty sure you just said that dude doesn't want to be locked down."

Shocked into silence, I turn my water glass around in my hands. "Well, what about you? You're trying to get rid of a guy so what are you doing wrong?"

"I don't know. That's just it. None of my usual crazy is working. I've done some of the most batshit stuff to this guy and he just... rolls with it." She looks annoyed.

"You should cook for him. Ask him about his day. Kiss him like you missed him. That should send him running. It works for me."

Her eyes light up. "That's it. We don't switch lives. We switch methods. I'll do things the Anya way. You do things the Ariana way. We both get what we want."

I blink several times. "Just start acting differently?"

"Nothing else has worked. So what have we got to lose?"

It's a tempting fantasy, that I can just transform into this confident, badass chick who demands what she wants but that's all it is. A fantasy. Real life doesn't work that way. I've always avoided drama and game-playing in my relationships and there's no way I'm changing that now.

"I'm going to talk to Law. We're adults, right? We should be able to have a calm, rational discussion about what we each need from our relationship." A text message lights up the screen of my phone.

JAMES LAWSON

**Where are you?**

"Crap, I have to go."

Ari smiles. "Good luck. And I'm not being shady when I say that. I actually hope it works out for you."

## LAW

AS I WATCH everyone move around the dance floor with the kind of reckless abandon that only comes with alcohol usage, I shudder internally.

God, I hate this shit.

Yeah, I know it's a bit of a cliché, the divorced dude who hates weddings. But it's not easy to pretend to be happy for people when you already know the dangers that await them.

Still, watching Andre and Casey move around the dance floor, I have to concede that maybe they'll be one of the lucky few that makes it.

I hope so, anyway. I may be a miserable bastard but that doesn't mean I'd wish it on anyone else.

Anya has been gone for a while so I send her a quick text message. We've been here long enough that hopefully no one will notice if we leave a little early.

"You're supposed to at least pretend to be happy at these things."

The voice over my shoulder sounds as bored as I feel. I glance over at the guy I recognize as the brother of the groom. He resembles Andre a little but has a thinner build and sharper features. Still, they both look like the kind of guys who belong on billboards.

Maybe men like that get a different ending.

He holds out his hand. "Philippe Lavin. I'm not sure if you remember me. I'm the brother of that sickeningly happy guy on the dance floor."

"I remember. You've been to the agency a few times for meetings. James Lawson."

"They're ridiculously happy." He inclines his head in Andre's direction and then chuckles.

It's an unfortunate moment to look since the bride and groom are currently kissing like they've forgotten anyone else is in the room.

"Yes, they are."

Apparently I haven't done a good job concealing my disgust because he raises his eyebrows. Belatedly I remember that this guy is the brother of one of my biggest clients so I can't wear my honest face right now. I need to have on my marketing agent, wheel-and-deal face.

"Marriage isn't for me but I wish them nothing but the best."

He shrugs. "It's funny, I used to feel the same way. But lately I've been thinking it might be nice to have someone to come home to. Someone who is happy to see me."

The look on his face is startlingly vulnerable and I clear my throat and look away.

Suddenly it feels too hot in the room and I tug at the collar of my suit. I need to get out of here before I suffocate from the weight of all the happiness and expectation in the room. It's a familiar feeling, one that brings back memories I'd rather not relive.

Because I've been that groom, flush with joy and overwhelmed with hope for a bright future.

Only to have to watch it all fall apart as the woman I loved morphed into someone I didn't recognize.

Philippe is watching me strangely now and I yank my hand away from my neck, suddenly aware I've been clutching my throat like I'm unable to breathe. It won't do to lose my cool in front of him.

Like it or not, I need the Lavin account to keep my agency afloat. The Mirage Agency is the only thing I have from my life before it all fell apart and I won't let anything threaten that. Especially not ghosts from the past.

"I thought that once, but take it from me buddy. If you want someone who is happy to see you when you come home, get a dog. It's cheaper."

I finish my champagne in one gulp and deposit the glass

on the tray of a passing waiter. It's time to find Anya so we can dance once and then get out of here. She's probably ready to leave, too.

I smile thinking of her wearing a bridesmaid dress that she hates. We understand each other and she doesn't like all this shit anymore than I do.

As if my thoughts have summoned her, Anya appears when a crowd of people move off the dance floor. When she sees me, her eyes light up. The joy in her expression makes me feel ten feet tall.

Watching her walk toward me calms the panic I always feel when I recall my marriage and subsequent divorce. I can't wait to get her out of here and back to my place where I can peel off that satin dress she hates so much.

Despite all my mistakes, I already have the perfect woman. She's smart, beautiful and has never asked for more than I can give.

Just uncomplicated, no-strings fun.

That's my idea of happily ever after.

When she reaches my side, she extends a hand. Tugging on it lightly I draw her against me as the band moves into a slow number. Anya sighs and rests her head on my shoulder.

The unmistakable smell of vodka wafts past my cheek and I chuckle. No wonder I couldn't find her for a while.

"I see you found the bar. Maybe I should have snuck out with you."

She smiles but it looks slightly strained. "I just needed to escape that stupid bouquet toss."

Then I understand. Weddings seem particularly designed to torture single women. Even though single men gather for the garter catch, no one gives you shit if you sit it out. Because no one really cares that much. Women don't seem to get that same consideration.

No wonder she left.

"We can get out of here in a bit. I think they're going to cut the cake soon."

She nods and her arms tighten around my neck. We dance like that in silence for a few minutes and just as the song changes to another slow melody, Anya gazes up at me.

"Do you ever think about where we'll be in a few years?"

There's something dangerous about the way she's looking at me right now. Any man who has been in a long term relationship or, I don't know, ever known a woman, is aware that the things they say often mean more than what they seem on the surface.

*How do I look?* translates to *Tell me I'm pretty.*

*What did you just say?* is roughly equivalent to *I'm giving you a chance to pretend you didn't just say that.*

Most importantly *I'm fine* never means *I'm fine.* Usually it means you've screwed up majorly and need to figure it out fast.

But all my years of experience give me no help translating what she means. Anya is usually pretty open about what she wants and is not the type to drop hints.

None of that is stopping my woman radar from going off.

*Danger ahead.*

*Danger ahead.*

*Proceed with caution.*

"Sure I do. I really think that Mirage will have expanded to more cities by then. You've always said that you want to travel more. Paris was fun, right? In a few years, we can do that all the time."

She sighs. "That sounds amazing. It'll be just you and me against the world."

"It's already you and me against the world."

"Maybe. I just wonder, don't you ever want more for us? Like this?" She looks around the room.

I follow her eyes to the bride and groom and what she's getting at finally dawns on me. "You don't like weddings," I stammer finally.

"No, I don't but I like what they represent. I don't need a big white dress. All I need is the two of us making promises. Making plans. Sharing everything, including a last name."

The shock of what she's saying makes me forget my footwork and we stumble slightly, bumping into the couple dancing next to us. I run a hand through my hair before searching for the door.

I have to get out of here.

Behind me, I hear Anya mutter a hasty "sorry" before she appears at my side, rushing to keep pace with me as we dodge the other couples on the dance floor.

I don't look at her as we make our way out of the ballroom and into the hallway. I can't come up with words to explain my reaction. Although just that makes me wonder.

Why should I have to explain myself?

I thought Anya got it.

I thought she got *me*.

"Law, what is wrong with you?"

We don't stop walking, but I acknowledge her with a quick shake of my head. "Not here. There are too many people."

She falls quiet with a little huff. The first room we come to is completely dark. I stick my head in and then keep walking. My luck we'd end up locked in a dark room and no one would find our bodies until next week. The room next to that has a party going as well. Probably another wedding. Then, a few doors down from the main ballroom, I find a smaller room with a few tables and chairs. It looks like it was being setup for some kind of meeting.

I can only hope we'll have privacy long enough for me to get to the bottom of Anya's sudden interest in the future.

"You're not going to make me forget what we were talking about. If that's what this little game of *Where's Waldo* is about."

Anya plops down in one of the chairs and crosses her arms. That's when I get my first glimpse of her face. She's really upset. I kneel in front of her and tug on one of her hands until she allows me to hold it.

"What's going on with you? You disappear to get drunk and now you're suddenly talking about getting married? Forgive me for being a little lost."

She looks sad for a moment and I think that scares me more than anything she's said so far.

Anya is relentlessly optimistic. In the office, she's an energetic dynamo that keeps us all organized and on schedule. After hours, she's the bright, spontaneous ray of sunshine that shines light into my life after years of thunderstorms. I never thought I'd feel hope for the future again but Anya brought me back into the world of the living.

The idea that she's not as happy with me as I am with her feels like being hit in the face with a frying pan.

"Law, are you happy with what we have? Just dating with no talk of the future? No labels and no commitment?"

My answer hovers on the tip of my tongue. It feels

reckless to tell the truth right now since what we have obviously isn't working for her.

"I don't want to lose you. You make me happy." My hope that honesty might be enough is dashed when her smile doesn't quite reach her eyes.

"I know. You make me happy, too. I was just wondering."

She no longer looks as sad but there's a resolute look in her eyes that's just as frightening.

"Let's go home, Anya. You're drunk and I'm tired. You can stay over and we'll make French toast tomorrow."

As I'm talking I'm inwardly disgusted with myself. I'm saying she can spend the night like it's a gift. I should be grateful a woman like her would even want to.

"Okay. Let me just say goodbye to Casey." She presses a soft kiss against my forehead before she stands and walks away.

I watch her go feeling like I narrowly missed getting hit by a train. But something tells me this particular train will be coming back for me at some point.

# *seven*

## ANYA

FOR THE PAST YEAR, Law and I have had a predictable pattern. We spend countless weeknights binging reality TV and many lazy Saturdays cooking or watching movies. Every weekend, I ignore the nagging warning sound in the back of my head and revel in the feeling of waking up in Law's arms.

Then every Sunday night, I head back to my place to get ready for work the next day.

It's a weird system but it works for us.

Until the day it doesn't.

"What's going on with you? Rough weekend?" Mya Taylor-Hamilton appears at the door to my office, the tablet she always carries clutched against her chest.

She's one of the VPs and a total marketing badass. Despite being one of the executives here and basically another boss, she also manages to be one of the nicest people at the same time. Not the easiest feat.

"Nothing! It's just ... Monday. I drank a bit too much this weekend." Clearly my concealer isn't doing a great job covering the effects of my sleepless night.

Going home is always a bit of a wakeup call but last night was worse than usual. My roommate, Jessi, forgot to throw away her takeout and there was a sour odor in the kitchen I couldn't get rid of even after I sprayed the room with air freshener. Smelling that definitely started my morning off on a bad note.

Jessi works at my favorite bar near the office. We became friends over the years and when my last roommate moved out, she was an ideal fit since she works nights as a bartender while she's finishing her Accounting degree. I spend so much time at Law's house that we barely see each other. Since I'm usually not there, it feels more like a storage center than an apartment.

Which is weird since I *definitely* don't live at Law's house.

Just imagining his response if I were to bring up moving in sends my mood right back into the basement.

She smiles in understanding. "Say no more. I've definitely been there."

I grin, probably a bit too widely, before pulling up the

calendar for the day. "You have a one o'clock appointment with a new client. I put you in Conference room 3."

"Yes. That's why I'm here. I was hoping you'd want to assist on this one. It's this cool new dating app that has everyone talking already." She wiggles in delight. "This is one of the biggest accounts I've ever landed for Mirage."

"I'm available to assist, Ms. Taylor!"

Mya rolls her eyes slightly before turning around. "Yes, I know. Anya, you've met Val before, right? She's one of the interns."

I nod and wave at Val. Mya campaigned to get an internship program started for ages before Law would finally approve it and he asked for my help verifying the resumes. Valor Wheaton came highly recommended by all of her college professors and has a 4.2 GPA.

"Why do you need more help? If you already have an intern, then it sounds like you've got it covered."

I really hope she has it covered because I'm not thrilled at the idea of working on a dating app. It'll just be one more thing that shows me how pathetic I am.

The people using that app will probably be married before I am.

"Because she just wants a chance to eyeball Seth Barrington."

The name sounds so familiar. I have a hazy image of a

handsome guy with intense eyes. "Seth Barrington? The finance guy?"

Mya grins. "That's the one. Washington DC's own Midas. Everything he does turns out making bank so we feel pretty damn good about this launch. I need someone with experience and not someone who is going to fangirl all over him."

Val shrugs sheepishly. "My major is marketing but I'm minoring in Finance. Seth Barrington is one of the guys we study in school. He is just like... goals."

Mya's shoulders drop. "Anya, I'm begging you. *Help*."

It's flattering that one of the top marketing agents has asked me to assist on so many campaigns. Maybe sinking my teeth into a juicy new project is exactly the distraction I need.

"So what's the deal with this dating app? How is it different from all the other ones?"

Mya looks smug. "Because this one helps you put your best foot forward. Most of these apps are just a meat market. You post a selfie and hope for the best. But if you aren't getting any results you have no idea why. This app pairs you with professionals to write your bio, photographers to take your profile photo and they even have career consultants on dial. It's like a dating app and a glam squad in one. It's brilliant."

"It sounds like it."

"Does that mean you'll be one of our beta testers?" Mya clutches her clipboard to her chest in excitement.

"What? Oh no. I'm just here to work."

"Okay."

She doesn't say anything else but I can tell from her tone of voice this is going to come up again.

Great.

"I'll do the beta test."

We both look over to see one of the junior agents, Wallace Burns, standing in the middle of the hallway.

His face flames bright red before he clears his throat. "I could use some help."

Mya's face softens. I think we both melt a little at the soft, bashful confession. Wallace comes across a bit bumbling but he's hardworking and really a sweet guy.

"Great. The more people we can get to try it out before the launch the better." Mya glances over at me and looks like she wants to say something else but settles for, "See you at one o'clock."

After Mya leaves, I turn around to find Wallace still standing there.

"Is everything okay?"

He shrugs. "Do you think people can really find someone from a dating app?"

"Anything is possible. I'll help you with your profile if you want. It'll be fun."

That finally brings a smile to his face.

"Thanks. There's this girl… but she only sees me as a friend. Maybe a little professional help could change that." With a wave, he goes back down the hallway toward the marketing cubicles.

Watching Wallace walk away, I'm suddenly brimming with ideas. Grabbing a notepad, I start jotting ideas and questions to show Mya later.

———

THE REST of the day flies by. To Val's disappointment Seth Barrington isn't at the initial meeting for GlowUp. We spend a productive three hours learning about the app, the background of the company producing it and start identifying key elements of the target market.

Everyone working on the campaign is invited to the app's soft launch party this weekend which leaves the whole office buzzing.

"There you are. I feel like I haven't seen you all day." Law appears at my side holding his laptop and a mug of coffee. It must have been a bad day if he's still drinking coffee at four pm.

"Mya had us in that new app meeting most of the afternoon."

He gives me a significant look and I glance around.

There's no one in the hallway so I follow him back to his office. As soon as the door closes behind us, Law nuzzles against me, kissing my neck.

And this, ladies and gentlemen, is why I can't get away. In theory it sounds so easy to just leave someone who can't give you what you need. But this feeling, this certainty that I am in the right place at the right time, no one else has ever given me that.

So what's a girl to do?

"We can't. What if someone comes looking for you? I can't be in your office with the door closed for long."

At work, we've tried to be discreet. I never thought I'd be that girl, the one banging the boss. My coworkers have never said anything but I'm pretty sure everyone knows. A fact I find mortifying at times but luckily no one has made comments about it.

At least not to my face.

"I know. It's just been a long day. Spent an hour on the phone with a new client trying to talk him off a ledge. His ads aren't performing as expected and he's freaking out. Then I had another HR meeting. You know how much I love those."

"That's why you're the boss. I hate boring meetings. And I am not the one to calm freaked out clients."

His eyes sparkle as he plants another kiss on my neck.

"He's a good guy. He's getting married this month so I should have expected this. Poor bastard."

I draw back at the barely hidden vitriol in his voice. "Why do you say it like that? Maybe he's happy."

Law scoffs. "Men don't get married to be happy. They do it because they don't have a choice."

Even though I knew he wasn't warm and fuzzy about marriage after his divorce, it never occurred to me that he just doesn't believe in marriage at all. This is a side of him I've never seen and that's probably partially my fault. Maybe I've been too scared to ask the obvious questions, justifying it as giving him space since he went through hell with his ex-wife.

But this is something entirely different.

And the time for looking the other way is over.

"So you're saying you don't think any married men are happy? They're all just dragged to the altar in chains?"

Law looks up from the papers he's been rummaging through on his desk. His eyes widen slightly as if he's just realized I'm upset and is baffled by it.

"No, of course not. I'm sure he's very happy."

"You could at least pretend you meant that."

Law sighs. "You know how I feel about this. It's just a piece of paper. People put far too much stock in it. Signing your name on a dotted line doesn't mean that you're going to live happily ever after. I know from experience."

He looks so frustrated that I want to back down but that's always what I do when we start talking about anything real. Maybe a year ago that was enough for me but ever since Casey's wedding, I can't pretend it doesn't matter anymore.

There's no shame in wanting a lifelong commitment and pretending like it's no big deal hasn't gotten me very far.

"You went through hell with Elizabeth. I know that."

"Do you, Anya? What do you really know?" Law looks pissed off now and I'm stunned by the nasty tone of voice.

"Only what you've told me. But one bad experience doesn't mean all marriages are bad. My parents have been married for almost thirty years. They're happy."

"With all due respect, you really don't know that. The only two people who know whether a marriage is happy are the people in it. Sometimes even they don't know. I sure as hell had no idea mine was going to blow up in my face."

"Okay maybe you're right. But they seem happy. Lots of married people I know seem happy. Do you really think all those guys are pretending? That's bullshit."

He wipes a hand over his face. "They just know they have to go along with it. Some women are marriage types and won't accept anything less. So they suck it up."

His words hit me like a truck. Is that what he thinks?

That I'm not the marriage type?

"So what does that make me, huh? One of those women who is willing to accept less?"

The room is completely silent as we stare at each other. Finally I turn away.

"Anya, wait. You're twisting my words all around. That's not what I was saying at all."

"I have to get back to work."

He looks like he wants to say something else but finally nods. "Right. I'll see you tonight."

Without responding, I walk out of his office making sure I have a calm, professional look on my face. When I get back to my office, I sit in my chair and start typing randomly on my computer. Hopefully I look busy enough that no one bothers me but I'm not seeing anything on my screen.

Instead my mind is replaying that conversation over and over.

Law thinks that all men only get married because they have to. Worse, he doesn't even see me as being one of the women worthy of this great sacrifice. There's no more pretending that eventually he'll want the same things that I do or that after he heals from his divorce he'll turn into the future husband of my dreams.

When I was younger, I always assumed I'd be married before I'm thirty. In all fairness, back then thirty seemed so far away. But it's almost here.

I can't put my head in the sand on this one.

The last two years I've been in some kind of la la land and it's time I wake the hell up. Law can't give me what I want and he never will. So I'm faced with a decision.

Continue with the status quo.

Or try something different.

*We don't switch lives. We switch methods. I'll do things the Anya way. You do things the Ariana way. We both get what we want.*

Biting my lip, I pull my phone from my purse. If I start down this road, there's no turning back. Ariana is like a bulldog with a bone when she gets an idea. So I have to be sure before I pull the pin on this grenade.

Honestly, I'm not even sure what she meant by her *do things the Ariana way* comment but whatever her plan is, it's sure to be aggressive, outrageous and pretty much batshit crazy.

Not that anything else has worked.

Milo and Mya walk by then. She's gesticulating wildly as she talks and he's staring down at her adoringly, like he's savoring every word.

That's what I want.

So I open up a new text message to Ariana.

ANYA PETROVA

Remember our convo at the wedding?

ARIANA SILVA

Refresh my memory.

I roll my eyes. Clearly it wasn't that revolutionary to her if she doesn't even remember.

ANYA PETROVA

The switching methods plan?

ARIANA SILVA

Let me guess, your man is acting up?

ANYA PETROVA

Something like that. Are you still up for it?

ARIANA SILVA

I'm always up for anything. I'm off today so come by after work. I have a feeling we need to act fast before you lose your nerve.

It's annoying that she already sees me as the weak link. Is that how I come across to my friends? As the desperate girl who can't get by without her man? Is that how Law sees me?

Maybe that's why he doesn't think I'm wife material.

Well that just fuels my resolve to do this.

ANYA PETROVA

I'm not backing out.

Law knows I'm not sick so I don't bother trying to pretend. Instead I quickly draft an email that says I have to go because one of my neighbors is locked out. I feel a little guilty about cutting out early but I can't let him cajole me into staying at his place tonight.

If I'm going to break free I have to rip the Bandaid off at some point so it might as well be now.

My coat is in the front closet so I quickly retrieve it and then make sure I have my phone and work badge before I press send on the message.

By the time he reads it, I'll already be in the parking garage and on my way to a new beginning.

ANYA

BY THE TIME I get to Ariana's apartment a half an hour later, I'm already frustrated. Parking in this neighborhood is always a beast and I almost got sideswiped by some jerk in an Audi who stole the first space I saw.

I'm ready to ask Ari where she keeps her vodka by the time I huff and puff my way up the stairs to the third floor.

Ari said she'd leave the door unlocked so I don't bother knocking. However, when I open the door, I immediately step back to be sure I have the right apartment. An elderly woman is at the stove and the air is thick with the smell of something delicious. She doesn't turn so I'm not sure she even heard me come in.

"Uh, hi? Is Ariana here?"

The older woman glances back briefly and then nods her head toward the hallway. Clearly that's her way of saying that Ariana will be right out, so I close the front door behind me and sit on the couch. A small black and white dog snoozes in a little bed in the corner.

I've been here before but usually there's a big group of us doing Girls' Night. It's not often I'm here during the day. Maybe Ari has an older family member who visits often and I've just never been here early enough to meet her. But it still seems odd that Ari didn't mention someone was here in her texts.

Then again, this is Ariana we're talking about. Odd is her normal.

A few minutes later Ari appears from the back holding a towel to her wet hair.

"Sorry about that. I've been doing some cleaning and really needed a shower." When she plops on the couch next to me, a shower of water droplets hits my arm.

Weird as it is, seeing her so disheveled actually makes me feel better. Even this supermodel lookalike is human it seems.

"So who is that cooking? Is that your grandma?" Even though the older woman is still in the kitchen I keep my voice low.

"Who? Oh no, that's Mrs. Abernathy. She lives down the hall. She cooks for me sometimes. I think she's just lonely."

Clearly I do a terrible job keeping the shock from my expression because Ariana chuckles.

"What? What was I supposed to do? Kick her out? I'm a bitch but even I'm not *completely* heartless. We can still talk. I'm pretty sure she can't hear half of what I'm saying anyway."

This is an unexpected side of Ariana but it definitely makes it easier to open up. Talking about my dating life with someone I don't know that well is already kind of weird but it's a lot easier with someone who has a soft spot for a lonely neighbor.

"Law and I had a fight. Maybe it's stupid but I really thought that eventually we'd end up at some kind of compromise. After today, I don't think that's going to happen."

Ari hums softly. "It happens to the best of us. You wanted to believe it would work."

"Yeah. But it's time I wake up. He doesn't want the same things that I do. So I need to make a change."

"What you need is some great sex."

My neck almost snaps at the conversational pivot.

"Not sure I'm ready for that. Besides, the sex was great with Law. If that's all I wanted then I would just stay with him."

"No, that's not what I mean. You don't *only* need great

sex. The reason you're unhappy is because you want more than that. But right now you're stuck in this rut because you think you can't find that chemistry with anyone else. We need to prove you can. You need to find a new source of great sex."

"How do you propose we do that? It's not like I can just Door Dash it."

"Yeah, I wish. Can you imagine if you could order great sex like fast food? Well, some of those names are kind of suggestive anyway. In-N-Out? *Five Guys*? What else would you need that many guys for?"

"Well, they're no competition for McDicks," I remind her.

"Booty King."

"Dick in the Box."

"Long John Ding-Dong." Ariana snorts with laughter as soon as she says it.

That's all it takes for both of us to lose it. Ariana howls with laughter until tears are streaming from her eyes. I'm not much better especially since I start giggling every time I think of how much Law loves Long John Silvers. Mrs. Abernathy turns around and gives us both a grumpy glare and I have to slap a hand over my mouth to quiet down.

Ari wipes the tears from her eyes. "I'm sure there's a great lesbian joke about tacos waiting to happen but I can't find it. I'm losing my touch."

Mrs. Abernathy carries over a tray with a platter of

something that looks like mini-doughnuts. The smell reaches my nostrils before she even sets it down. I'm reaching for one before I can remind myself about the diet I'm supposed to be on.

Whatever. I guess I'll start over next week.

"I'm disappointed. You missed a great opportunity to say Dick-Fil-A," Mrs. Abernathy comments in a raspy voice that makes me feel like I need to clear my own throat.

Ari's hand pauses mid-air with a doughnut dangling. "You heard that?"

She grunts. "There's nothing wrong with my hearing. I just don't care to listen to most people's bullshit."

We watch in silence as she ambles to the front door and grabs the cane leaning against the wall. A second later, the door slams behind her as she leaves.

Ari yells, "I'm starting to understand why your family doesn't visit!"

The cackle of laughter that comes back makes us both smile.

"Okay that was hilarious. Also these fried doughnut things are really good." I take another and munch happily.

There's nothing like sweet, carb-heavy delights when you're having a crisis.

"She's cranky but she's a great cook." Anya licks her fingers and then leans back on the couch. "Maybe there's a lesson in there for you."

I pause mid-chew. "A lesson that I need to be more cranky?"

"Not exactly. More assertive? Possibly."

Being more assertive? Not likely. I'm sure it's not that hard to be a go-getter if you have a strong personality like Ariana but for me, not so much. It's a huge part of why I'm such a great office manager. I like making sure everyone has what they need. I'm a people pleaser. I always have been.

That's not going to change easily.

"Well, I told Law that his *all men hate marriage* theory was bullshit. Then I left. That's about as assertive as I get."

Suddenly I get a mental image of me as a doormat while Law wipes his shoes on me. I thought I was sticking up for myself by walking out today but really, what did that accomplish? I didn't even tell him I was leaving face-to-face, instead sending an email like a coward.

No doubt Law is just going to ignore the whole thing until I lose steam and forgive him. Isn't that the way things always go?

"Hey now, don't look like that. I wasn't saying that as a bad thing." Ariana grins. "I'm just pointing out our starting point. That's why you're here, right?"

"I'm here because I have no idea what I'm doing."

"Not true. Mya always says you have more energy than the rest of the office combined and that you keep track of a million details without breaking a sweat. All we have to do is channel that badassery on your behalf. We are going to organize the hell out of your dating life."

Her energy is contagious and I push my shoulders back, ready to banish this blah feeling. Ari's right. I use my multitasking prowess for everyone else everyday. It's time I use a little bit of that mojo for myself.

"I'm not sure I have much of a dating life to work with but I'm game."

Ariana holds up her hand for a high five. "Yes. Now the first thing you do when you clean up is take out the trash."

It takes a minute before I understand her point but once it's out there, it hangs over my head like a raincloud.

"Yeah. I guess it's time. And after that?"

Ari tilts her head thinking. "We need to figure out how to ease you back into single life. I'm not sure if you'd like the club scene. Maybe we should start smaller, like going out for drinks."

Remembering Mya's request this afternoon, I take a deep breath.

Out of the frying pan and into the fire.

"What about the launch party for the hottest new dating app? Want to be my date?"

Ariana laughs. "Hell yeah. But if I have my way, you definitely won't be coming home with me."

I DON'T SEND the text to Law until I'm at home. Maybe I thought the extra time would help me figure out how to do it but in the end, I go with the usual crap.

*We need to take a break.*

*I need some space.*

These are standards for a reason. Short. To the point. Non-accusatory while still being clear.

The phone rings and Law's picture flashes on the screen. With a sigh, I silence the call. I can't talk to him right now. If I talk to him, he'll just convince me to come over and I'll end up backtracking.

No. I get up, determined to find something productive to do. Despite just flushing the last two years of my life down the toilet, I refuse to wallow. I still have a life to lead. There are chores to be done and other people who need me.

However, as I clean my apartment, it's obvious that the main person who needed me has now left a conspicuously large hole in my life. The time after work I'd usually spend at the grocery store and planning our dinner is now filled with washing clothes and reorganizing my closet. The evening that would normally be spent with Law hanging out or making love is now going to be just me on my couch.

Frantically I try to remember whether I canceled my cable.

Crap. I did.

Okay so the evening will now be spent figuring out all

the ways I've neglected my own place while spending so much time with Law.

It's while in the middle of sorting through a month's worth of mail that it finally hits me.

We're really done.

The tears that threaten infuriate me. Why am I crying over a man that doesn't want me? Correction, he wants me for sex but not for life. I may have spent the last year in fantasyland but now my feet are firmly on the ground. There's nothing wrong with casual sex if that's what both people want but I want more. It's time I started behaving accordingly.

By the time I get to work the next morning, I've given myself five different pep talks, including one to keep me from calling in sick. I refuse to allow Law to think I'm at home desperate and sad because of him.

As Ariana reminded me, I have options. It's time I start using them.

"Morning, Anya. After you get settled, can you come help me in the conference room?" Mya tosses this over her shoulder as she whirls past my office door.

"Sure thing."

I'm grateful she's in a hurry this morning and doesn't have time to scrutinize how I look. She's got an eagle eye for more than just amazing advertising. I take a moment to check my appearance with my phone camera.

Hopefully the effects of the crying jag I gave into this morning in a weak moment aren't written all over my face. After stashing my stuff in my desk, I walk down the hall to the first conference room.

Mya leans over her husband's shoulder, pointing at something on the tablet he's holding. "This could be brighter. Yeah, exactly. We need to punch it up. You know how picky he is."

"Is that the new Lavin ad campaign?" I ask as I move closer.

Mya smirks. "What gave it away?"

We all share a chuckle. Andre is notoriously difficult when he doesn't like something. It's so weird to think he's now married to one of my best friends. Law has spent many evenings raging about how many man-hours have been spent on his campaigns.

I pinch my arm. *No thinking about Law.*

"Is he coming here today? Wait, that's a dumb question. They're probably still on their honeymoon."

"Yes, they are. But apparently that doesn't mean he's not working. So we're going forward with the focus groups we talked about last night." At my blank look, she frowns. "The focus groups that James suggested. Didn't he tell you?"

"Right. Of course. Let me just grab my tablet with all my notes on it. I'll be right back."

Mya's eyes follow me as I leave the conference room. I

press the backs of my hands to my cheeks, hoping I'm not as red in the face as I feel. It's day one and I'm already hitting a roadblock in my plan.

*Get it together.*

Luckily I don't encounter anyone else on my way back to my office. Glancing around quickly to confirm I'm alone, I pull out my phone and send a quick text to Ariana. If I'm going along with this plan of hers, then the least she can do is talk me down when I'm flailing.

ANYA PETROVA

I'm already falling off the wagon on this plan.

Immediately I see the blinking cursor indicating that she's typing something.

ARIANA SILVA

What? It's only been a day!

ANYA PETROVA

How am I supposed to avoid him when he's my boss?

ARIANA SILVA

Fair point. Okay maybe you can't avoid him but that doesn't mean you have to kiss his ass either. Be professional. No chit chat. Work and then go home.

ANYA PETROVA

Easy for you to say. This love shit is hard.

ARIANA SILVA

Nothing about love has been easy for me.

Normally I would have been all over that cryptic statement but when Milo walks past my open door, I hastily stuff my phone back in my bag. I don't have time for a quarter-life crisis right now.

Work ethic is one of the things I've always prided myself on. This past year in particular, I've gotten to be a part of some really cool things. I love my job and I refuse to let a man take that away from me.

I take a deep breath and then pull out my tablet to find the notes I made during the last Lavin campaign meeting. When I look up, Law is standing on the other side of the desk watching me with a wary expression. My heart tumbles a little at the sight of him.

He looks tired. The faint lines on the outside of his eyes that I've always thought were cute are more pronounced than usual. My first instinct is to ask if he's okay or if he needs some of the Tylenol I keep stashed in my desk for when he gets a headache.

Then Ariana's words flash in my mind.

*Be professional. No chit chat.*

"Good morning, Mr. Lawson."

His jaw drops and then he glances behind him as if looking for who I'm talking to. My lips want to curl into a smile but I keep the same bland, disinterested expression when he turns around.

"Seriously, Anya? You didn't call me back yesterday and now you're acting like we don't even know each other."

"I'm acting like you're my boss."

He's about to say something else when Mya walks up. Seeing her arrival as the opportunity it is, I hold up my tablet.

"I've got my notes. Sorry for the delay."

Mya glances between us as if she can feel the tension but then nods. "Great. Let's get started. I want to get this completed before lunchtime since I have another meeting."

"Excellent."

I gather my things, avoiding Sharon's curious gaze as Law follows us down the hallway past the reception desk.

Keeping our personal problems out of the office is going to be a real challenge, yet another reminder of why banging your boss is a monumentally bad idea. Not only is it weird for everyone around you since they can feel the tension but also it's just plain torture having to see your ex throughout the day.

I groan when I remember that one of the things on my agenda for this week is to screen junior marketing agent applications. Another thing that's going to force me to deal with Law since he usually interviews all new hires.

"Anya, we need to talk about this."

His serious expression would be funny if it wasn't way too little too late.

"What is there to talk about? It's not like we disagree about what to order for dinner."

"That's not what I'm saying. I just don't understand what's changed."

Seeing Mya waiting at the end of the hallway, I paste on the most professional smile I can manage.

"Everything."

He looks like he wants to say something else but then he glances around like he's just remembered we aren't alone.

"We'll talk about this tonight."

## LAW

CLICKING through page after page of search results, I'm no closer to finding the perfect gift than I was an hour ago.

What says *I love you but I don't want to get married?*

Funny. Google doesn't have an answer for that one.

The worst part is I'm stymied not only by my lack of search results but also by Anya's behavior. Lately she's two parts bulldog and one part fluffy, emotional marshmallow. That's a combination I have no idea how to navigate. This is not the Anya I know. The focused, driven, happy woman who never lets anything stop her or slow her down.

So what's changed?

*You. That's what changed. She got involved with you.*

It's a depressing thought.

"Excuse me, Mr. Lawson?"

The door to my office is partially open and Wallace

sticks his head in. I hold in a groan. He's a nice kid and a hard worker but I'm not in the mood for one of his circular, picking-my-brain sessions tonight.

"Actually, I was just on my way out. Walk with me?"

As I speak, I close the lid of my laptop and then grab my briefcase from the floor. At least if we're on the way to the parking garage, I have an escape plan if Wallace gets too long-winded.

"Right. I just wanted to say thanks for approving my request to switch to Mya's team."

As I hit the button for the elevator, I try to remember when I approved his request. He was on Milo's team before and I don't recall there being any problems.

"Of course. We want you to be happy."

That seems to please Wallace because he launches into a long description of his first day. By the time we reach the parking deck my head is already starting to pound.

"Anyway, I think I've found my niche and working on GlowUp has been really exciting."

"Fantastic."

When the elevator doors open, I head straight to my car giving Wallace a wave over my shoulder. Maybe if I stop at a grocery store on the way home I can get some flowers and chocolates.

When I pull into the driveway, I'm surprised to find it

empty. Anya wasn't in her office when I left so I expected her to arrive first.

Once I unlock the door, I drop my briefcase in the front hall and kick off my shoes. It's no big deal. Anya was working on the Lavin account all afternoon so she's probably staying late to wrap things up. Whatever the case, it must be taking longer than expected.

Not that I can't keep myself busy. I tidy the room, making sure to put the flowers in a vase on the counter. Anya loves red roses so I got three dozen. I figure it can't hurt to make a big statement.

When nine o'clock comes and goes, I finally give in and eat a microwave pizza. I turn on the local sports news and sit down on the couch to wait.

I wake suddenly, glancing around the room warily. I'm sprawled across the couch with a throw pillow tucked under my head. My half-eaten slice of pizza is still on the coffee table. The clock on the wall reads 11:36 p.m.

"Anya? Are you here?"

Rising slowly, I ignore the lingering ache in my back from sleeping in that weird position as I walk back to the bedroom.

It's empty.

I take out my phone and send a quick text. Immediately I see the little dots indicating that she's typing. Then they disappear. My patience gone, I hit the button to call.

"Law, it's the middle of the night."

"Yeah, I know. I was waiting for you."

"I told you there was nothing to talk about."

My brain is still sluggish from sleep so it takes me a minute to process. I knew she was mad but I didn't think that meant she wasn't coming. Anya is the most easygoing person I know. Even when she's mad at me, she can't maintain it for long.

"I was worried when you didn't show up."

"There's no need to worry about me. I'm a big girl. I'm in my pajamas reading a book."

The mental image of her cozy in bed and perfectly fine makes my own disheveled state even more offensive. Apparently she's completely fine with this sudden disruption to our schedule.

"So, you're not coming?"

"No. I'm not coming."

Panic rises and it feels like the back of my throat is closing up. This feels different than the other times we've fought. There's something in her voice that makes me feel the need to drive over there right now, hour of night be damned. But considering the mood she's in there's no guarantee she'd even open the door.

"Okay, tomorrow then."

She sighs. "Not tomorrow either. I have plans."

"Plans? What kind of plans?"

"Does it matter? After all, it's not like you're my husband."

Then she hangs up, leaving me wondering what the hell just happened to my uncomplicated life.

"Okay then."

I open the fridge, thinking a snack will help and I'm greeted by a whole lot of empty space. There's barely any food inside. I try to remember the last time I went grocery shopping.

I can't remember.

Then I think of all the times Anya has shown up with grocery bags. I used to tease her about hoarding food like a doomsday prepper.

*Not so funny now, huh?*

The pantry isn't much better but I'm able to find a loaf of bread that luckily doesn't have mold on it. Toast will have to do for a midnight snack.

But as I stand at the counter a few minutes later chewing the dry bread, I sincerely hope this isn't a metaphor for how my life is going to be from now on.

———

THE NEXT MORNING I arrive at the office late. It feels like a million eyes are on my back when I finally push through the glass double doors leading into the agency. This is the first time in five years that I've gotten here past eight o'clock.

That's what happens when you can't find your shoes and you almost run out of gas on the highway and have to stop at a random station.

"Morning, Mr. Lawson!" Sharon calls out as I pass by.

I respond with a quick wave and hope she doesn't take offense. As I cross the threshold into my office, I let out a sigh of relief.

Then promptly spill my gas station coffee all over my desk.

"Jesus! What is it with this morning?"

"Hey, boss. Is everything okay?" Wallace sticks his head in the door.

*"Does it look like everything is okay?"*

His eyes widen as he looks between me and the mess all over the desk. "Uh, not really."

He backs out of the room slowly. A minute later he returns with a roll of paper towels.

Which of course makes me feel like shit.

I accept the offering gratefully, feeling even worse about how short I was with him. I take a few deep breaths. It's not his fault and I don't want to take my shitty mood out on everyone else.

"Thank you."

"No problem." He fidgets, shifting from foot to foot while I clean the desk.

"Did you need something?"

Now that my desk is clean, if a little sticky, I try to focus on why we're all here. Work has always been my haven and it never lets me down. It never leaves me to sleep cold and alone with nothing but toast for company.

"No. I mean, maybe. Do I look okay? I mean, how do I look?" Wallace stops fidgeting finally but then starts tugging at his tie.

He's wearing a nicer suit than usual and his hair looks like it's been gelled back. Business casual is our standard unless we have a client meeting so this sudden GQ look is a bit of a departure for Wallace.

"You look great. What's the occasion?" I mentally scan over the last few staff meetings. Is there something going on that I missed?

Just then there's a commotion in the hallway. A bunch of people I recognize from the accounting department walk by in a flurry of chatter. Wallace suddenly looks green.

"It's the GlowUp campaign meeting. All the beta testers are invited to talk about the launch party on Saturday." He tugs at his tie again knocking it askew.

I reach over and straighten it. "You look great. There's no need to be nervous. It's just Mya and a few people from other departments, rights?"

We walk out into the hallway together and I'm stunned by the crowd heading into the conference room. This many people signed up for the beta test? Several young women walk by that I swear I've never even seen before.

"Who are all these people?"

Wallace looks over. "Mya recruited a pretty large test group. The investors were really impressed. Some of these girls are just here for Seth Barrington though. He's supposed to be coming today."

Anya walks by then and she stops when she sees Wallace. Keeping her eyes on him, she smiles. "Looking good! Are you ready for this?"

He nods. "Yeah. Yup. Totally not nervous at all."

Anya still doesn't look at me. "Just stick by me. We'll do it together."

That's when I notice her outfit. She's wearing this black wrap dress thing that looks new. And low cut. Her short black bob has been styled messily and to my horror makes her look like she's just climbed out of bed after having sex. She's also rimmed her eyes with some kind of black stuff that makes them look even bluer.

In short, she looks completely and totally fuckable.

"Wait? Anya, you're going? Isn't this just for the people doing the beta test?"

Clearly I didn't do a good job sounding professional because Wallace clears his throat.

"I'll see you in there, Anya." He ducks between us and then walks into the conference room.

Anya turns to follow him but I step into her path. She rolls her eyes.

"Did you need something, Mr. Lawson?"

My growl startles us both. *"Would you stop with the Mr. Lawson crap?"*

"I'm just trying to do my job. Can you move? The meeting is about to start and I don't want to miss anything."

Why do I suddenly feel like I'm trapped underwater? It's hard to breathe and my heart rate rises so fast I get lightheaded.

"So you're actually..."

"Doing the beta test? Yes."

"Anya, what the hell?"

"What, Law? What is the problem?"

She keeps her voice low but one of the junior agents passing by glances over at us warily. She puts a hand up to stop me before I can say anything else.

"I'm not doing this right now. What I *am* doing is going to a launch meeting for GlowUp, a promising new dating app. After all, if I'm not wife material then I shouldn't be acting like a wife. I'm in my twenties so I should be out partying and sleeping around, right?"

"First you stop talking to me, then you blow me off last night and now this?"

She shakes her head. "Law, I didn't blow you off last night. *I ended things* last night. You get that, right? Or did you think I'd be mad for a night and then get over it like I usually do?"

Stunned, I can't even respond. I wouldn't have thought it was possible but as the silence stretches between us, she looks even more angry. Then she closes her eyes.

"Wow. You really don't think I have a backbone at all."

Shaking her head, she walks past me. All I can do is watch helplessly as she joins the throng of people in the conference room. I follow, glaring at one of the associates until he moves and makes room for me to stand behind her.

Mya whistles and the room quiets. Then she gestures to a tall, dark-haired man standing at her side.

"Everyone here already knows the chief investor behind GlowUp but for anyone living under a rock, I'd like to introduce Seth Barrington. Mr. Barrington has graciously come to tell us about his vision for the app. Let's all listen and learn."

I've seen pictures of him before, of course, but I didn't recall him being that tall. Or that handsome.

As if she can read my thoughts, Anya looks over her shoulder. "I have a feeling I'm going to learn a lot."

## ANYA

BEFORE NOW, I would have never believed how long a week could be. Pretending Law is invisible made each day feel like an eternity.

The office has shrunk to the size of a matchbox if the number of times he passes by my open office door is any indication. Every coffee break requires the planning and stealth of a secret mission. At least I have access to his calendar so I know when he's busy but that doesn't stop him from randomly popping up places I don't expect him to be.

Every time it's an effort not to respond to the sadness in his eyes. However, I've managed to stay strong so far. We won't mention all the junk food I've been stress eating all the while.

It's either Snickers or sex.

A girl only has so much willpower.

Now it's go time and I'm running out of bravado fast. The GlowUp beta launch party seemed like the perfect place to debut my *get-over-Law* plan but now that I'm here, I'm starting to panic. After a lot of debate, Mya chose to book *Les Printemps*, this super fancy French restaurant, for the party. It's the perfect venue to communicate the vibe she wanted, elegant and exclusive but still fresh and fun.

I got here early to help with the setup but now it's almost time for people to start arriving and I'm rethinking everything. Especially what I'm wearing.

The little black dress that seemed like the conservative choice when I grabbed it this morning doesn't seem so safe now that I've changed clothes. Clearly I didn't take into account the weight I've gained stress eating because my boobs are trying to make a break for it out of the neckline.

Finally the door opens and Ariana appears. I let out the breath I didn't realize I was holding.

"There you are! I was starting to think you were going to stand me up."

She stops mid-stride and makes a huge production of looking me over from head-to-toe.

"You look *hot*."

Her wolf whistle makes me blush a little. Especially since she looks stunning as always in a red bodycon dress that makes her legs look about eight feet long.

"Stop it. I'm nervous enough already."

Ari winks. "You have nothing to be nervous about."

"Yes, I do! I have no idea what I'm doing and this stupid dress is too short. Plus I've eaten my weight in chocolate this week. Maybe this is a bad idea."

I can hear myself whining and wish I could staple my lips shut. But now that we're here and people are starting to arrive decked out in their "looking to get laid" outfits, it's getting real. I'm supposed to meet someone tonight.

A man.

Who will expect me to talk to him and maybe at some point in the future get naked?

*Oh god.*

My stomach rolls and I'm suddenly sure all the chocolate I've eaten today is going to make an appearance.

"I think I'm going to barf."

"You need to chill. Come here." Ari grabs my hand and tugs me to the corner of the room.

It feels like everyone is staring at us and there's a huge neon sign over my head that says "chicken shit".

"Oh good. There's no one in here."

I follow her behind a counter and into what turns out to be a coat closet. She leaves the door open a little so we can see. It's weird being in this closet in the dark but getting away from all the prying eyes helps.

"Take a deep breath. This is supposed to be fun."

"Fun? Can't we have fun at my place eating ice cream?"

Perfectly tousled blond curls fly around her face as she shakes her head. "Uh uh. Do not give up. *Do not let him win.*"

"Easy for you to say. You just like chaos."

"Yeah kinda. At least I can admit it. What about you? You had a really good reason for wanting to make a change. That's what you need to remember tonight. Why are you really doing this?"

"Law doesn't think I'm wife material." The words slip out before I can think of a lie.

Something about Ari is like truth serum.

"Hmm. He's dumber than I thought because you are totally wifey. I can picture you baking cookies and wrangling kids in a perfect little house with a white picket fence."

"I'm not sure if you're making fun of me or not."

"This is my honest opinion. Scouts honor." At my dubious look, she grins. "Okay, you got me. I was never a scout."

"Yeah, that's a shocker."

"But the point is that you are a badass boss babe. You have a lot to offer. Just because *one* man doesn't understand how lucky he was doesn't mean you go home and give up. You are going to go out there and have a good time."

"You're right."

"Damn straight I'm right." She pauses. "Just out of curiosity which part am I right about?"

"The badass babe part. I have a lot going for me. I am great at my job. I have money in my account. Well...some. I'm bilingual."

"See! That's impressive stuff."

"Well, okay my Russian actually kind of stinks but I can understand it. That counts, right?"

"I tell people that I speak Spanish and Swedish. Really I just understand my parents when they complain about each other in their native languages. So it definitely counts."

She adjusts the neckline of my dress, yanking the spaghetti straps up slightly to lift my cleavage. "Look at us. We're like a hot version of the United Nations right now."

"Yeah we're bringing world peace." I roll my eyes.

She slaps me on the ass playfully. "Now get out there and work it!"

The door to the closet opens and the sudden bright light makes us both squint. It takes a few seconds but my brain finally registers the identity of the man staring at us. Perfectly tailored suit. Intense dark eyes. Chiseled jaw. The faint aroma of billions.

Seth Barrington is hard to forget.

"Hey. You're interrupting our hot girl on girl action here!" Ari puts her hands on her hips and sends him a saucy grin.

After a shocked pause, Seth laughs. It's a pleasant sound, deep and rumbling, but it's hesitant, almost like he's forgotten how. There's something about him that makes him seem almost sad. He has the air of a much older man who has been through some stuff and doesn't trust anyone.

Maybe it's the way people always seem to want something from him. I noticed it at the office. People treat him like either a god or an ATM. That has to get old.

"Please don't stop on my account."

Ari preens under the attention. "The mood is gone. Come on, Anya. We have a mission."

I follow Ari out of the closet, feeling exposed now that we're venturing into the crowd. My earlier bravado is waning and it's hitting me that I actually have to talk to people tonight.

*Men.* I have to talk to *men* tonight.

"Good luck," Seth calls out after us.

I glance back over my shoulder to meet his eyes. The way he stares without wavering sends a little chill of pleasure over my nerves. It's unnerving to be the center of such intense focus.

"Okay. What do we do now?"

While we were in the closet, a lot more people have arrived. Mya will be thrilled. Her efforts to hype this party up as the place to be this weekend clearly worked.

"The mission is to get a date with someone before the

night is over. You're supposed to be a bad girl. So go make bad decisions."

"You're awfully bossy. Just what are you going to do?"

Ariana smooths her hair. "I'm going to be good tonight."

———

WITH A SMILE AND A WAVE, Ari disappears into the crowd leaving me on my own. I take a deep breath.

*It's time to make it happen.*

The mental image of a cheerleader with a bullhorn makes me smile. Only I could make mingling at a party this dramatic.

But I'm used to being in situations where I have an express purpose. At work I have a list of tasks to accomplish and talking to people is easy when I'm trying to help them. Talking about... whatever people talk about at parties is an entirely different thing.

My eyes land on the buffet tables. Mya wanted a catered affair but because she had to organize the party so fast, she'd gone with a buffet. As I wander over to the tables, I'm grateful she made that decision. Getting a plate of food gives me something to do instead of standing in the corner looking awkward.

There's a guy there staring at the warming containers of chicken breasts. I figure that's a safe choice but then I notice it's covered in a cream sauce that looks like it has mushrooms in it.

"Mushrooms? No thanks," I comment, glancing at the guy from the corner of my eye.

He looks over and grins. "Exactly. I've been standing here for way too long trying to find something to eat. No caviar or French snails for me, please."

I laugh at the exaggerated face of disgust he makes. See, this isn't so hard? Wait until Ari sees me. It's only been a few minutes and I've already found someone to talk to who seems nice. And cute, too.

I take a few surreptitious glances at him while he continues to peruse the offerings. Brown hair that looks messy in that adorable way men have of styling it. Dark brown eyes with lashes long enough to make me envious. He's wearing a navy blue suit with no tie, a look I've always enjoyed on men. Dressy but comfortable.

Like the kind of guy who knows how to be serious when necessary but how to have a good time, too.

"Are you having fun so far?"

I have to raise my voice a little over the music and then cringe at how boring the question sounds.

Couldn't I have come up with something a little more original? I might as well have asked him what his sign is or whether he comes here often.

Luckily he doesn't seem to care, just plunks a piece of

steak on his plate. "Yeah, this is awesome. Free food and an open bar feels like my kind of party."

"Me too. Maybe–"

Whatever I was about to say dies in my throat when a beautiful girl with long red hair appears at his elbow. She looks vaguely familiar.

"Babe, are you doing okay? Sorry, I know this is boring but we don't have to stay long." Her eyes land on me and then she grins. "I know you! From the marketing agency, right?"

Instantly I remember seeing her at the launch meeting. She had her hair up in a bun and was wearing glasses.

"You're one of the developers working on the app, right?"

She nods absently before taking one of the mini egg rolls off her boyfriend's plate. "Mmm. Yeah, we're all here tonight to make sure there aren't any issues. Brilliant idea to put sign up stations right here at the party, by the way."

"I think so, too. Mya knows her stuff." I smile weakly as they walk away leaving me holding an empty plate.

Okay, so attempt number one was a fail but that's okay. Mushroom guy was just practice. I'm sure there are plenty of guys in the crowd who are actually single and not just here for the free food and booze.

I take a few fried mozzarella sticks and then some kind

of tomato salad. Just when I take a bite, someone stands next to me.

I look over and see a guy with long, messy blond hair. He raises his glass.

"Hey. What's up?"

With a mouth full of fried cheese, there's not much I can do other than give an awkward half-wave. He doesn't seem to need much encouragement though as he moves closer to peer at the other stuff on my plate. A little too close for comfort actually.

Is this normal? Maybe I'm being too picky but I don't like the idea of someone breathing on my food.

"That tomato salad is good but dairy is really bad for you." He squints at the mozzarella sticks.

I swallow. "Guess that means you won't be asking for one then, huh?"

He looks confused. "Dairy causes a lot of inflammation."

"*Right.*" I move away slightly, ready to take my bad food in the other direction.

Who comes up to a stranger to give them a diet lecture?

There's a group of people nearby so I casually position myself on the outskirts of their group. Maybe if I look like I have friends already I can avoid some of the weirdos. I'd rather observe people first before trying to start a conversation. Then I can make sure they're eating normal food and aren't here with a girlfriend.

One of the guys in the group is standing kind of on the edges also, only occasionally making a comment to the things his friends are saying. He seems normal enough, so I decide to give it another try.

"Do you guys work for the app?"

He shakes his head. "My friend's little sister told us about this party. I signed up. It sounds fun."

So far so good.

"It should be great. I like that they have professionals to help with your profile. Sometimes people just need a little assistance to reach their potential, you know?"

Suddenly he smiles widely, looking way more animated than before. "Exactly! I used to say that all the time. My friends don't get it. We're all capable of so much if we just have a little help."

His intensity is a little surprising but at least he seems friendly enough.

"I totally agree." I smile back, determined to be positive and open to a new friend.

"Just the other day I was saying there's so much more to this world than what our conscious mind can comprehend. It's mind-blowing." He makes a blowing up motion with his hands, glancing over at me as he does it.

My smile feels frozen on my face. "Right. Mind-blowing."

"If you just take care of your body, you can unlock so many hidden levels to your physical energy. If you're interested in achieving your best, let me tell you about this yoni tea. I have an amazing opportunity for a self-starter on my team if you're interesting in unlocking the full power of your feminine energy."

Of course. In a room full of people I manage to pick the ringleader of an MLM scam.

"Thanks but my *yoni* is perfectly fine. And feminine."

I leave my empty plate on one of the standing tables and search the room for Ariana. There's no way this is going to work for another hour. I might as well just admit to her that I failed and go home. Just then a handsome man with dark hair turns around and I stop in my tracks.

It's the guy from the wedding. The one who had to give me the Heimlich.

Nope. Nope. Nope.

I immediately turn in the other direction but have to stop again when I notice Law talking to a group of men a few feet away. Anxious, I glance to the left but all I can see is yoni-health dude coming my way again.

A panicked giggle rises in the back of my throat. It's raining men. Except it's all the men I don't want to see.

I walk toward the front of the restaurant. The closet that

Ariana and I were in before is still unmanned so I send up a prayer that the restaurant didn't feel the need to hire a coat check for this event. I need a place to hide out.

With the door partially open there's just enough light for me to see so I don't crash into the rack of coats in the middle of the room. Thumbing through the rack, I see a Burberry trench, a Gucci coat and some kind of wrap that has Halston sewn into the lining.

Wow. Were all these items really left behind by patrons of the restaurant?

I can't imagine having so much money you don't care about leaving your designer coat behind.

As I move the items around, I notice the room extends quite a bit behind the rack. If I push the coats to the left and right there will be enough space for me to step through to the other side. After sliding the coats back in place, no one will be able to see I'm there. Which is perfect in case yoni-dude comes looking in here.

Still holding the Gucci coat, I shove the others out of the way and tentatively step through. A sharp tug pulls at my scalp.

"Ouch!"

I reach up and feel several strands of my hair caught on a zipper. Twisting slightly I manage to pull the lock of hair free and then almost trip over the metal rung at the bottom of the rack. I place the Gucci coat back and pull the others in place around it to close the gap.

Then I turn around and jump so high I almost hit the ceiling.

*"What are you doing in here?"*

Seth Barrington looks up from his phone and shrugs. He's sitting on a small stool in the corner and looks like he's been here for a while.

"Probably the same thing you're doing in here."

I narrow my eyes. "This is starting to feel deliberate."

"Well, in my defense, I was here first this time."

"Touché."

My sigh seems loud in the room. It's more than a little awkward standing in such a confined space but Seth shows no signs of moving and I'm definitely not leaving.

"I'm hiding," I blurt out.

Instantly his face changes. "Is someone bothering you? Because if they are, let me know."

"No. Not like that. I'm hiding from a handsome man. He's not the one bothering me anyway. That's another guy."

His brows lift. "Sounds complicated."

"You have no idea. Anyway, the handsome guy, not the other guy... well, actually they're *both* handsome."

Seth laughs softly. "I'm going to need a flow chart to follow this story."

Now I'm laughing, too. "The first handsome guy I don't

really know that well. But the last time he saw me I was choking on something."

Seth's eyes glint. "Is that right?"

All at once I realize how pervy that sounded.

"Not like that!" My face flames with embarrassment but I can't stop laughing.

He shakes his head playfully. "You said you were choking on something? What could you have meant? Was it meat?"

I slap a hand over my mouth. We've pretty much blown our cover by being so loud at this point but I can't stop. Seth seems to enjoy the fact that I can't control myself, watching with undisguised amusement.

Suddenly the door to the closet flies open and someone pushes aside the coats blocking us from view.

Law glances between us, his jaw tight. "My apologies. I thought this was a coat closet."

The unspoken censure in his gaze is obvious. Seth tenses next to me and I get the feeling that a little space is a great idea.

"No problem. We were just leaving. You ready?" I look over my shoulder at Seth, wondering if he's going to play along.

He hesitates for a beat before nodding. "Whenever you are."

LAW

WATCHING their backs as they walk away, it takes all of my patience to remain in place. Decking a client in full view of all of my employees, at the client's own party no less, is probably not the best way to keep my business afloat.

But when Seth's hand dips low on Anya's bare back, all my thoughts of patience and self-restraint go out the window.

*"That motherfu–"*

A hand clamps down on my shoulder, holding me in place. I turn, ready to swing on the person stupid enough to get in my way but lose some steam when I see Milo's grin.

"What are you smiling about?"

"Nothing. Let's just say I feel your pain but this really isn't the time to make a scene."

It's tempting to pretend I don't know what he's talking

about but when I turn around to see if Seth is still groping Anya in public, the two are nowhere to be found.

They're probably hiding in another closet somewhere.

"Are you okay or should I stick around?" Milo gestures with his drink toward the back of the room. "Otherwise I should probably go circulate. Make sure our clients are having fun."

I wave him off, ignoring the sense of shame his words bring up. This is my company. GlowUp is a major campaign for us. Instead of working the room and generating potential new leads, I'm sulking in the corner like a toddler whose favorite toy has been taken away. It's hard to ignore my emotions but that's the job. When you own a business you can't just think about yourself. Mirage has to be the best not just for me but for all the employees who rely on their paychecks for survival.

This is why I don't do commitments. No emotion. It just gets in the way of what's really important.

"I thought you just hated weddings. Now, I'm starting to think you hate people in general."

The sly voice at my side is a surprise.

"Philippe Lavin. I'm surprised to see you here."

The other man accepts a glass of champagne from a passing waiter. As usual, he's wearing what looks to be a custom made suit, no doubt from his brother's line. I wonder idly if he ever wears anything else. I've never seen him in casual clothes or anything that doesn't look custom tailored.

"I'm an investor in the GlowUp app."

My face must convey my surprise because he chuckles before taking an appreciative sip of his champagne.

"Milo mentioned the app when Seth first started looking for investors. I'm not just my brother's keeper."

Even though his voice remains even, there's something beneath the surface that makes me wonder if all is well in the Lavin world. As happy as he always seems, being second fiddle to your brother has to be a difficult position at times. I certainly can't blame the lesser known Lavin for wanting to invest on his own.

"We're glad to have you on board another venture, Mr. Lavin. Let's hope the app's official launch to the public is as successful as this party."

His eyebrows raise slightly, almost as if he's thinking about challenging the bullshit that just came out of my mouth. In the end, he just nods and then moves on. We're both stuck between a rock and a hard place, forced to put on a happy face and I think we understand each other.

Looking around the room, I see that Anya and Seth still haven't reappeared. Just as I'm about to go check every other closet in this place, Mya appears looking frazzled.

"James, there you are! I've been searching all over."

"Is everything okay? The party seems to be going well."

As annoyed as I may be at the founder of GlowUp, I can't deny that this launch party was a great idea.

Initially I'd been skeptical but Mya has proven herself once again. There has been nothing typical or overdone about this launch. Just in the time I've been here, I've seen quite a few people creating profiles at the computers lining the walls and the "selfie stations" Mya insisted on have been in use all night.

"Yes, it's great. But this isn't about the party."

A crowd of people passes by in a cloud of noise and confusion so I follow her out of the way. She glances around warily before beckoning me closer.

"I just got a phone call. From Elizabeth."

Suddenly all the noise in the room fades into the background. Her name shouldn't still have the power to steal the breath from my lungs but yet here I am, breathless.

Even after ruining my life she still has power over me.

"Why is Elizabeth calling you? I didn't think you were friends." I don't mean for it to come out accusatory but Mya lifts a brow in reproach.

"Sorry. I know you wouldn't do anything shady. I was just surprised."

"It's okay. No, we're definitely not friends but apparently she's been trying to get in contact with you. Since you changed your number, I guess she's calling everyone who knows you. My number is on our website."

Although I don't want to ask, pretending not to care isn't going to fool Mya. Or anyone, really.

"Is she okay?"

"She just left a message. I wasn't even going to tell you about it but then she kept calling. It must be pretty important."

"I'll call her and see what's going on."

She nods. "Okay. I hope I did the right thing telling you."

"You did. No matter what she's up to, the last thing I want is her harassing my employees. I'll handle her. You just focus on the event. Great job on a successful launch party, by the way."

Her smile is genuine. "Thanks. I'll go see if Mr. Barrington wants to say a few words before we wrap things up."

"Could you let me know when you find him?"

At her shocked look, I realize my voice is suddenly very loud. I clear my throat.

"I'd like to congratulate him before the night is over. That's all."

"Of course. I'm sure he'd appreciate knowing the owner of the agency is giving his account so much personal attention."

Yeah, personal attention.

*I'm pretty sure he's getting lots of up close and personal attention from Anya right now.*

Before anyone else has a chance to ask me anything or otherwise interfere, I retreat to the corner and then bring up my phone app. Deleting all of her information was more of a symbolic gesture than anything else. I don't need a contact on my phone to remember the number I used to dial everyday. There was a time when Elizabeth was my favorite person to talk to.

Sure, I could be petty and refuse to call her back but what would that really prove? Especially since I know I won't get any rest until I know what's wrong with her.

What if she's sick?

Or in some kind of trouble?

She hurt me but the emotions that come from being married for so long didn't disappear the day we signed our divorce papers.

So I dial the number I still know by heart.

———

AN HOUR LATER, I'm sitting outside the restaurant, uncaring if the rough concrete beneath my ass is ruining the fabric of my suit pants.

Who cares about what I look like when my entire world has just been turned upside down?

The party has started to peter out at this point because I can see that a few people are still inside. Hazy shapes move back and forth behind the front window like dark spectres. From out here, it looks warm and welcoming, a sharp contrast to the cold bite of the wind that whips around me. But I can't seem to get myself together to go back inside.

Will people be able to tell that I'm a broken man when they see me? How will I shake hands and talk shop when all I can think about are the four words that keep echoing inside my head. And the other four words that knocked me on my ass.

*I made a mistake.*

*I want you back.*

The door to the restaurant opens again but this time instead of another group of inebriated young women, Anya steps out onto the curb. She turns toward the parking lot, wrapping her coat closer around her body against the wind. Then she notices me and her steps slow.

"Law? What are you doing sitting on the ground?" She peers at me closely before lowering her voice. "Are you drunk?"

I grunt. "Not drunk enough."

Anya looks like she's about to walk off. Probably to go meet up with her new billionaire boyfriend.

"I was looking for you earlier. I need to talk to you."

She sighs. "We can talk at the office on Monday."

The thought of a long, lonely weekend without her is unimaginable. When she first pulled away, I thought this would be a phase and she'd eventually be as tired of the pretense as I was. But she seems completely unaffected by our time apart.

Does she even miss me?

How is she so calm?

"Now you won't even talk to me outside of business hours? Like I'm just another coworker?"

Anya looks sad. "You are just another coworker."

"This is bullshit! We've been together for two years. How can you just walk away like it was nothing? Like you don't even care."

She spins around. "No, you don't get to do that. I cared. All I have done these past two years is care. But you only want me around when it's convenient. Despite what you think, I deserve more than that. I deserve it all."

"You think a man like Seth Barrington is what you need? What kind of promises did he make? Is the billionaire playboy supposed to be your knight in shining armor now?"

She sniffs and dabs at her eyes. "I don't know but at least now I have the chance to find out."

The thought of him touching her makes me want to rage. Especially when I know his type. Rich, brilliant and used to getting whatever he wants, he'll string her along with pretty promises and then leave when he gets bored.

"You don't even know him."

"I'll get to know him. That's what dating is about." She rolls her eyes and turns to walk away again.

"So he'll get to be with you because he's willing to do what I won't. Lie. He'll say whatever he thinks you want to hear. Doesn't honesty count for anything? All I've ever done is try to protect you. I don't want to hurt you."

Anya pauses and when she looks back, the tears on her cheeks shock me into silence.

"You say you don't want to hurt me but *this* is hurting me. If you can't give me what I need, then the kindest thing to do is let me find someone who can."

When she walks away this time, I let her go.

# twelve

ANYA

IT'S NOT until Monday morning that I realize I never got around to making a GlowUp account at the party. Glancing around, I open the app on my phone. Not that I think anyone here would care that I'm using it during work hours. It's for a client, after all.

*Liar. You can think of one person who wouldn't be happy to see you using it.*

Thoughts of Law are the last thing I need when I'm trying to ramp myself up to fill out a dating profile. The whole thing feels so weird. You would think being on the arm of the guest of honor at the party would have given me some confidence. I smile thinking of Seth. After the closet confrontation he'd suggested we get a drink. People approached him constantly but I noticed he would stand closer whenever it was a woman.

If you'd told me ahead of time I'd end up being an anti-wingman for a billionaire, I would have asked what you were smoking.

And whether I could have some.

The fact that it made Law jealous should have been a bonus. Instead I'd gone home feeling slightly sick. I close the app without doing anything. Maybe I should have waited until after work when Ariana could help me.

I send her a text and then my phone lights up. She's calling me.

"Hey, what's up?" I keep my voice low so no one outside my office will hear. I could close the door but that would probably draw more attention than anything else.

"Hallelujah! You're finally ready to get this party started."

"I guess. I went to the launch party to mess with Law's head but I didn't actually think I'd make a profile. All these dating apps seem like such a meat market."

"What's wrong with that?"

"Seriously? It's just a bunch of dudes looking for a place to stick it."

"That's what you want, right? Sex, no strings. Have some fun, get out there and see what you've been missing. You might find *The One* or maybe you'll just have a bunch of orgasms. Let's see."

I can hear her typing but I'm not sure what she's doing.

"So, about that profile... I already made one for you."

"You did *what*? Oh god, I'm almost scared to ask what you put on there."

Ariana cackle-laughs and despite everything, her exuberance makes me smile.

"I did a great job. I think I really captured your soul."

"Send me the link to it."

After a minute, a link pops up in our message chain along with the login details Ariana created. When I click it, the GlowUp app opens again. I log in and then navigate to my new profile. A picture of me with my tongue sticking out and my bra strap showing is the first thing I see.

"Ari, what the hell? What is this picture?"

"It's great, right? You look cute as hell."

"I'm not even looking at the camera. And why is my shirt falling off?"

"It's cute and playful. You look like fun."

"I look like I'm coming off a five-day bender."

That's when I notice the rest of the profile. I was so caught on the horrible photo that I missed the description. The "About Me" section says, *New to the scene. Ready for some peen. Show me what I'm missing.*

"Ready for some peen? Oh my god, how many people have seen this!"

She makes a shushing sound. "Calm your tits, chica. It's only been live for a few minutes. I didn't make it public until just now. I made it at the party so you'd be ready to go whenever you made up your mind."

"Well, how do I take it down? I don't want every mouth breather in the DC area sending me dick picks! And I need a better picture."

Switching to the camera app, I start taking selfies. It would have been nice to have some notice so I could have worn something more exciting than a white button down shirt and tweed skirt. It's fine. Anything would be better than that busted photo.

The app makes a chiming sound.

Then another.

Ariana guffaws. "What is that I hear? Sounds like a good time!"

Then she hangs up.

I click the red flags popping up at the bottom of the app. My eyes bug out. Five matches. Five people actually liked that crappy profile? My head drops into my hands. This whole thing is a little overwhelming. For the last few years, I've heard from friends nothing but horror stories about dating apps.

A notification pops up on my computer for my next meeting. I close the app and put my phone in my pocket. Now probably isn't the best time to dive into the waters of lewd pickup lines and gross dick pics. I grab the tablet I use to take notes and head for conference room B.

By the time I get there, Mya, Kevin, Val and Law are already waiting.

What is he doing here? He wasn't scheduled to be in this meeting.

"Morning." I make cursory eye contact with the others and then direct my attention to the screen at the front of the room.

"Okay everyone, let's go over our initial data from the first batch of GlowUp beta testers." Mya clicks to change the slide in her presentation and the image changes to a pie chart.

Movement across the table grabs my attention. Law holds up his phone and mouths something. Immediately, I turn back to the front. The slide has changed again to something with a bunch of percentages on it.

Law clears his throat. Loudly.

Mya stumbles over her words and glances at him in alarm before continuing. Once she's not looking, I glare at him.

*Stop*, I mouth.

He holds up his phone again.

It's a struggle to pay attention when I can see him moving but I deliberately keep my focus on the presentation. I can only hope that Mya doesn't ask for my opinions on anything since I have no idea what's going on.

Just then my phone starts chiming again. Everyone looks at me.

Crap.

"Sorry. I thought I put it on silent." I take my phone out and click the volume button on the side furiously.

"That sounds like the GlowUp notification. Are you using the app?" Mya asks excitedly.

Acutely aware of the man sitting right across the table, I nod slightly.

"Excellent! What do you like about it so far? Have you experienced any of these issues?" She clicks back in her presentation and brings up the pie chart slide again.

The table jolts when Law stands suddenly. Mya watches mutely as he walks out. Kevin looks at me and then pointedly turns his attention to the table in front of him.

Right. Because that wasn't obvious at all.

"Um, I haven't noticed any issues." I slide lower in my seat as Mya continues her presentation, desperately hoping she doesn't ask me anything else.

As soon as we're done, I grab my tablet and practically run toward my office. Down the hall, I see Law waiting outside the door. Turning to my left, I duck into the ladies bathroom. Hopefully he didn't see me.

A second later, a text pops up on my phone.

JAMES LAWSON

Now you're hiding in the bathroom to
avoid me?

My thumbs hover over the screen. Should I respond or pretend I don't see this? Before I can answer, a new calendar notification pops up. Law has set up a meeting for us on his work calendar that is marked Urgent.

As annoying as it is, I have to admire his persistence. Before I can accept the meeting request, another text pops up on my phone.

JAMES LAWSON

Unless you're willing to ignore your next
payday, I expect to see you in my office.

Ugh. Resigned to my fate, I put my phone in my pocket and leave the bathroom. His office is at the other end of the hall from mine so I take my sweet time getting there, stopping in the employee break room for another cup of coffee. Someone brought in donuts and left them on the counter so I take one for good measure.

By the time I get to Law's office, I'm halfway through eating it and have white powder all over my fingers.

"Nice of you to show up to do your job today," Law grumbles as I sit in the chair in front of his desk.

"Just participating in a little office socialization. Donuts do a lot for morale."

"Noted. Can we work, please? We need to go over the office budget for next year."

Okay now I feel a little guilty that I wasted time getting here when he's actually got work that needs to be done. Maybe he's not the only one having trouble keeping our personal life out of the office.

For the next half hour, he talks and I take notes. After working together for so long, we have a good rhythm and we finish the new budget and a few client pitch drafts for each of the three team leads. We take a break and Law rests his head on the back of his office chair.

"So you're using GlowUp?" he asks in a deceptively soft voice. "What happened to your new boyfriend?"

"Nothing happened to him. He is a very nice man but I am keeping my options open. I have to evaluate the app to help the marketing team."

"The marketing team," he says bitterly.

"And to help myself. Maybe I'll get lucky and find someone who wants the same things I want."

"What you want doesn't exist." He still isn't looking at me.

"I think it does. Honesty definitely exists. Loyalty is a little harder to find."

"If that's what you want then you're walking the wrong way."

"You'll have to excuse me if I want to investigate that for

myself. Men aren't the best at directions. Besides that's not all I want."

His eyes fix on mine, the intensity enough to take my breath away. "You want late night conversations where you feel free to say anything. Evenings wrapped around a man who doesn't want to be anywhere but where you are. You want adventure and excitement, safety and comfort, and everything in between. Most of all you want to know that you can let go and someone will be there to catch you."

My heart bangs against my ribs. It feels like a warning.

It's not just the husky tone of his voice as he spells out the secret wishes of my heart that break me. It's the look in his eyes, like he's aware that he's the only man who has ever come close to giving me that.

"Don't forget never-ending brunch," I whisper. "French toast and bacon are a crucial part of my happiness."

"I haven't forgotten. Not a single thing."

Someone walks by in the hallway and the sound of loud voices outside the closed door breaks the spell. I glance down at my lap, not sure why I suddenly feel like I've lost something precious all over again.

My phone screen flashes. After my earlier mortification I made sure to turn the sound off but I kept the notifications on. I pick it up and check the screen. The jaunty little GlowUp notification tells me that I have new matches waiting.

Law sits up in his chair, his eyes narrowing when he notices the phone in my hand.

"Good luck finding Prince Charming."

Even though it's tempting, I refuse to rise to his bait. Arguing about the merits of dating is useless and doesn't solve anything.

While he watches, I tap the app to open it. Hmm. Just over the last hour, I've gotten three more matches. One catches my eye immediately. The guy is wearing a blue baseball cap and has decent biceps on display in a short-sleeved shirt. I click his profile and look it over.

"I don't know about Prince Charming but this guy seems promising. A shy guy who likes surfing and rescue dogs sounds perfect for me. And he's already asking for a date. I like a man who takes initiative." I type a quick message back to "Shy Clint" telling him that I would love to meet up this weekend.

Law walks around the desk. He stands behind me as I finish typing.

"Are you done?"

Confused, I nod.

Then he leans down and takes the phone out of my hand. He looks at the profile as if he's evaluating the guy's potential.

"Checking out the competition?"

I'm going for bravado but it's making me intensely

uncomfortable to see him holding my phone in his large hand. His thumb strokes over the screen as he scrolls down and I shiver. He dips his head and his breath brushes against the side of my neck.

"Do you think our friend Clint here will figure out how much you like having your hair pulled?"

When did he get so close? My fingers clench around the armrests of the chair.

"I'm sure he will eventually. If I decide I like him that much."

He's still leaning over me looking at the profile but I've forgotten all about poor Clint and his slightly above average biceps. Because all I can focus on is the skin exposed where Law has rolled his sleeves up. He's not an overly bulky guy but he has always worked out regularly. However, I don't remember his forearms being this muscular before.

Did I just miss that or is this some sort of sex-withdrawal symptom?

"Let's hope our friend pays enough attention to notice that your ears are particularly sensitive."

I moan softly as his lips graze my ear. Involuntarily my eyes close as the sensation travels all the way down my spine. He isn't exaggerating about how much I love it when he pays attention to that area. Once during sex, he bit my earlobe softly and I came like a rocket. The memory alone has me wet.

When I open my eyes, his gaze is so incendiary that I'm shocked the entire room hasn't gone up in flames.

I know that look.

"Law, what are you doing?" I whisper, but I already know what's about to happen.

"Your neck is all I can think about. All day long when I'm supposed to be thinking about clients, payroll or any number of things, all I can remember is how soft your skin is right below your jaw. How it tastes."

His hands land on the arms of the chair, caging me in. The heat of his body surrounds me and when I take a deep breath, all I can smell is him.

I'm fighting a losing battle and I know it.

"We can't do this."

His hand threads through my hair and when he pulls at the back, my eyes almost roll in the back of my head. With a gentle tug, I'm out of my seat and plastered to his chest.

As soon as our lips meet, every thought I had about why we shouldn't do this is lost. In that moment, all I want is his taste on my lips and his hands all over my body. My legs wrap around his waist when he lifts me, carrying me a few feet to set me on the edge of his desk. We don't separate the whole time, our tongues tangling as his fingers dig into the underside of my ass.

"Christ, Anya. If you knew how much I want you." He sounds almost angry as his hands tug at his belt buckle.

I gasp, trying to catch my breath but as soon as he shoves his pants down, he's kissing me again. He lifts me and his hands slide under my skirt. I pant as he tugs my panties down in one swift motion.

It shouldn't be so hot how easily he's manhandling me but there's no point denying it turns me on. I'm sure the panties he just tore off me are soaked.

He thrusts once and immediately I shudder at the invasion. Like he's just as affected, he pauses and rests his forehead against mine.

"Fuck, yes. That's what I want. Right there."

"Right there," I echo and he opens his eyes.

Holding my gaze, he starts to move and the friction immediately sends me right to the edge. It's unbearable not to make any noise when I'm splintering apart from the inside out but I'm trying. After one ragged moan escapes, Law covers my mouth.

The carnality of his hand over my lips silencing my moans while he slowly fucks me on his desk proves to be too much.

The pleasure snaps and I gasp through rolling waves that threaten to pull me under. As my muscles clench around him, Law's face twists into a grimace that looks almost painful. His lips cover mine and he moans into my mouth, one long sound that makes me ache inside all over again.

He moves back and instantly the cold air in the room makes me shiver. We don't look at each other as we each shift our clothes around and try not to look like two people who just had desperate sex on a desk. His eyes follow me as I pick up my panties from the floor and step back into them.

The awkwardness drives home how different things are now. There was a time I could say or do anything with Law without worry. Now every little thing is fraught with tension. I mourn the loss of that ease between us as much as the physical part.

"It doesn't have to mean anything." The words sound hollow even as I say them.

"Just breakup sex, huh?"

The look he gives me says he knows I'm full of shit. Despite the fact that he's right, it pisses me off. Like he's so sure it's only a matter of time before I give up and come back to him.

There's no mirror in Law's office so I can't check my appearance. I settle for running my hands over my hair a few times and tucking the stray pieces behind my ears. I grab my phone and tablet. I'm not sure whether we were actually done working but anything else will have to be handled over email. There's only so much I can deal with in one day.

Law doesn't say anything as I gather my stuff but I can feel his eyes on me the whole time.

Right when I reach the door, I look back.

His eyes lock on mine, like he's daring me to admit our mid-day hookup is proof I'm not ready to move on. What he doesn't get is that sex has nothing to do with why I left him. Our chemistry isn't going to make me forget what's missing between us.

"It's not breakup sex. You were never my boyfriend, remember?"

———

THE REST of the week I don't even have to try to avoid Law. He stays in his office with the door closed and I make myself very busy tackling the backlog of supply requests from each department. Not that our mutual avoidance keeps everyone else from noticing the weirdness.

Mya has suddenly stopped asking me for anything that would involve Law and even Sharon asked why the boss is mad at me. I'm sure it won't be long before someone fills her in as to *exactly* why.

Shame burns my cheeks as I think of all the conversations in the break room that have suddenly died when I walked in the last few days.

All the work that's piled up should keep my mind from what happened in Law's office but by the time Friday arrives, I've given up on being productive. Our office hookup completely threw me off my game. When I catch myself staring off into space reliving the moment his palm covered my mouth for the sixth time, I decide it's time to get my weekend started.

It's not even four o'clock but that's close enough. It's Friday so whatever.

Friday. Date Night.

I groan. Agreeing to this date with "Shy Clint" was probably a mistake.

It was an impulsive move to piss Law off but do I really want to go clubbing with some guy I don't know? Maybe I should have suggested something less intense like meeting for coffee. If he's a creep then I'll be stuck with him for hours if we're at a club.

Ariana insisted that I get ready at her place. Before I leave the parking garage I make sure I have my garment bag with my dress and my only pair of black high heels that don't pinch my toes. They might not be as cute as some of my others but I refuse to spend a night dancing in uncomfortable shoes.

"You're early," Ari comments as she opens the door a few minutes later. She's wearing a faded shirt and leggings with holes in them and holding a can of soda.

I step into the living room and drop my bag next to the couch. Now that I'm away from the office, the stress I've been feeling all week finally falls away. It's crazy how much energy pretending to be fine takes.

"I left early. I had to get out of there."

"Bad day with the boss-ex?" Ari takes a loud slurp of her soda.

"Sex on the desk with the boss-ex."

She chokes. "Maybe you should have left earlier."

That makes me laugh.

"Not today. It was a few days ago. Now things are even more awkward. People around the office are starting to gossip."

"You don't know that for sure, right?"

"The new receptionist asked me what was up with me and the boss. So... yeah."

"Ugh, sorry."

Something pink and glittery catches my eye. There's a long ribbon dangling from the ceiling. Weird but then again, this is Ariana. She's the type to decorate with random ribbons just because.

However, it drives home how one-sided our conversations have been. Instantly I feel like a crappy friend. We've been conspiring for the past two weeks on this whole GlowUp thing and I've never once asked about how things are going for her.

"So how are you? Are you still trying to get rid of your guy?"

Suddenly she looks guilty. "About that. Yeah, I think he's here to stay."

"That's great! I guess that means he won you over."

"You could say that. I didn't want to say anything since it technically means I broke our pact."

I feel bad that Ariana felt like she couldn't tell me about what's going on in her life. Breaking up with Law wasn't about a drunken pact at a wedding. It was about taking control of my life and figuring out what I ultimately want.

The whole reason I'm doing all this is so I can feel good about where I'm heading and why. That includes the people I'm spending time with.

"The pact was about us getting what we want." I take a seat at the counter next to her. "Is he the one you want?"

She shrugs but I can see how happy she is. Her whole face practically glows just at the thought of him.

"He's taking me to meet his mom tonight." She takes another slurp of her soda.

My eyes land on the drink in her hand.

Ari chuckles. "Sorry. I'm kind of nervous. I've never done the whole *meet the mom* thing. Anyway, do you want one? I probably should have asked. I'm new to the hostess thing."

"It's fine. We're just hanging out. I could do with some water though." When she starts to get up, I wave her off. "I can get it."

"Make yourself at home."

When I open the fridge my eyes immediately go to a large sheet cake that is partially sticking out of a brown paper bag. Is that... a cake shaped like a pair of boobs?

"Are you having a party?" I point to the ribbon on the ceiling and then inside the fridge.

Ari jumps off her barstool. "Sorry. I forgot that was in there."

She moves past me and pulls the brown paper bag over the cake. I decide not to ask. This is awkward enough.

Besides I'm not sure I really want to know what kind of weird party Ariana might be throwing.

When she turns around, she regards me for a long moment.

"There are some things I want to tell you. But not now. I'm really enjoying hanging out with you and not having to think about anything other than fun stuff. If I talk about certain things, then it makes it real. Does that make sense?"

My throat tightens because I have a sudden idea what the boob cake is about. As my eyes meet hers, I suck back the emotional response. We may not know each other that well, but these past few weeks it's been a lifesaver to talk to someone who isn't also friends with Law.

I can completely understand wanting someone to talk to who doesn't know your baggage.

"No worries. I get it."

Over the next two hours, Ari not only loans me a dress (after declaring my choice tragic) but does my makeup, including a bold winged liner that makes me look fierce as hell. While I'm doing my best to style my limp hair, my phone chimes.

She puts out her hand. "It's probably your date. Let me answer him."

When I hesitate, she chuckles.

"I'm going to suggest a place for you to meet. This new club called *Spectrum* is amazing and I know one of the bouncers. When his wife went into labor early, their daughter was in the NICU for almost a month. He's a good guy and he'll keep an eye on things."

Ari is a nurse and used to work in the neonatal unit. She started working in the Emergency department after some tough cases. I can't imagine having premature babies under my care every day so I understood the switch.

I unlock my phone and hand it to her. She types while I swipe a little more gel through the top of my hair. If it frizzes with all this product in it then it's a lost cause anyway.

"Okay, you're all set. Also I accepted a coffee date with another guy for tomorrow morning. You're welcome."

My eyes widen. "Just throw me in the deep end, huh?"

"If this date is a dud, you need to get right back on the

horse. No wasted time." Ari hands me the phone and then takes a critical look at my hair.

"Am I making a mistake? This guy could be a serial killer."

She ignores my grumbling and swipes a piece of my hair to the side. "You're taking a chance. That's never a mistake. Besides you can always call me if things go south and you need an immediate extraction."

"Same goes to you. If the mother turns out to be a nightmare, let me know and I can call with a dramatic fake emergency."

Ariana laughs. "She'll probably need the fake emergency to get away from me."

# thirteen

## LAW

WHEN I STARTED MY BUSINESS, I had
nothing more than a few hundred dollars in my account and
a prayer. That business now employs more than fifty people
and has an impressive roster of Fortune 500 clients. Every
year I run a 10k for charity. I own my own home.

I'm not incompetent.

Glaring down at the burnt chicken in the pan, I decide
not to even bother trying to figure out where things went
wrong.

"I can cook my own damn dinner," I grumble.

The sound of the fire alarm going off breaks my
concentration. With a flick of my wrist, I turn off the burner
under the pan and then grab a magazine to fan the smoke.
The alarm continues blaring for another minute before it
finally falls silent.

After a brief inspection, it's clear the chicken isn't that far gone just heavily seared. The only part that's really burnt is the very bottom. Maybe I can scrape that off. Plating it with the microwave rice I made earlier, it looks decent.

It doesn't look like the elaborate dinners Anya used to create but it's edible. I sit down at the dining table, deliberately ignoring the empty place setting to my left. Anya used to prop her feet in my lap while we ate and tell me all the office gossip that no one else would ever say to my face. Then afterward we'd clean up together.

Those were some of my favorite times. We didn't need to talk to feel connected. It was enough just to look over and see her there.

"This is a perfectly nice evening."

I'm not sure who I'm trying to convince but I take a defiant bite of the chicken and chew methodically. My jaw is sore after struggling through a few rubbery pieces.

Maybe it was seared a bit more than I thought.

When the phone rings, I almost break my neck answering it. It's barely done with the first ring before I have the receiver at my ear.

"Hello?"

"Oh hey. I wasn't expecting you to actually answer," my brother says. "I know how Anya feels about her dinner time."

"Yeah."

He groans. "What did you do?"

"Why are you assuming that I did something? Maybe she got a job offer in Alaska? Maybe I decided to become a Tibetan monk and live in solitude?"

"Let me guess," Thomas says.

"Please don't."

He continues as if I haven't spoken. "That nice girl got tired of waiting around for you to get your head out of your ass."

The accuracy is insulting.

"That's not what happened."

He laughs. "*Right.* I seriously don't get it. Yes, you got kicked in the nuts by Liz but that doesn't mean you just give up on life."

"I'm not giving up on life. I'm eating dinner."

There's a loud commotion and I hear Thomas yelling at one of the kids.

"I thought you were going to be a cool dad this time around."

"Screw that. I don't have the patience. But we're not talking about me."

"Aren't we? You seem to think I'm desperate for a different life, Tommy. News for you, little brother, not everyone wants the white picket fence ending. But I'm glad it worked out for you."

"That's true. This life isn't for everyone. But if that's what she wants, you need to let her go so she can find it. I know you'll do the right thing. You always do. Even if you're completely clueless about how to do it."

"Thank you, Oprah. Was there a reason you called or did you just want to bust my balls?"

"That's reason enough, jackass. *Oh shit, take that out of your mouth!*" There's dead air for a few seconds before the call drops.

"Yeah, I'm really missing out on that domestic bliss."

Before I sit down again, I decide I need music. No wonder I feel so strange sitting here alone. It's too quiet. I turn on a classic rock playlist and the sound comes through the portable speakers in the kitchen. I carry one of them back into the dining room with me. Just as I'm about to sit down, a text message pops up on my phone.

ANYA PETROVA

I'll see you at Club Spectrum at 9. Can't wait to meet you!

My brow furrows. What is this? But before I can respond, I see the little bubbles moving indicating that she's typing again.

ANYA PETROVA

Sorry. Wrong person.

I wait, wondering if she'll say anything else. Maybe one of the same things I'm thinking.

*How are you?*

*I miss you.*

*Let's stop this craziness and get back together.*

Then I read over the message she accidentally sent. My jaw clenches at the "can't wait to meet you" part. Did she send this as a passive aggressive way to shove her new dating life in my face?

Well, she's in for a surprise.

I don't care.

At all.

I sit down and take another bite of my chicken. The music continues playing in the background and I move my head to the beat. Then I get up and grab a beer from the fridge, twisting off the cap with a practiced flick of the wrist. I'm just a single guy enjoying a nice dinner with a beer.

Five minutes later, I take my plate into the kitchen and cover it with plastic wrap. Then I call Ethan.

He answers immediately. "Lawson! What's up, man? I hope you're not working on a Friday night. I heard about the Sayer account."

"Yeah, their account rep hasn't confirmed why they passed. I know our presentation was top notch. But anyway, that's not why I called. I need you to meet me somewhere."

"Um, okay. Where?"

"This club called *Spectrum.* Have you heard of it?"

He laughs. "*You* want to go to *Spectrum?*"

Something about the way he says it makes me bristle. Why does everyone assume I'm so boring?

"Yes. It's not like this is the first time I've ever been clubbing."

Ethan is still laughing. "You've been there a lot, huh?"

"Sure. It's great."

That sends him into another fit of laughter. "Okay. Any particular reason you want me to come clubbing with you on a Friday night with no advance notice?"

*To keep me out of jail.*

"No. Why do I need a reason to hang out with one of my oldest friends?"

Just before I hang up, I hear him grumble, "*Why does everyone always call me with their bullshit?*"

———

I'VE BEEN SITTING PARKED on a side street near *Spectrum* for more than fifteen minutes waiting for Ethan to show up. Clearly when I said *meet me* I should have clarified that I meant *right fucking now.*

Finally Ethan texts that he's here. I get out of my car and follow the sidewalk around the building to where the long line to get into the club starts. Shit. I should have been standing in line while I was waiting for Ethan to arrive. This is going to take forever.

It's already after ten o'clock.

Ethan falls into step next to me. "Hey man. Sorry it took me so long."

I don't want to yell at the guy when he's helping me out. Sending Ethan to scope things out is the perfect plan. He can make sure Anya is okay and if she sees him she'll just think he's out clubbing.

Then I have the mental image of Anya being groped by some guy. Ethan won't want to get involved. He'll just tell me that she's on a date and it's none of our business.

The fact that he's right is irrelevant. I *need* to see what's going on in there.

"Okay what's the plan?"

"I just figured we could hang out."

His eyes narrow. "You want to hang out with me suddenly on a Friday night at a specific club? A club I *know* you've never been to before."

"Yes. What's wrong with that? We're friends. Just two single guys going out to have a good time." I pause. "How do you know I've never been here before?"

"Right. Whatever, dude. Come on."

We bypass the line and I glance over my shoulder at the people who are glaring at us. Ethan walks right up to the bouncer and gives him some kind of fist bump. Then we're being shown inside. The music is so loud my ears hurt as soon as we walk in.

"How did you get us in?" I yell over the music.

Ethan smiles sheepishly. "I used to party."

That's probably the short answer to a long story but I don't have time to wonder what kind of shit he gets into in his free time. I have to find Anya. It's dark in here and there's some kind of weird strobe light that makes everything look purple. There are a lot of people in here.

How the hell am I supposed to find anyone in this crowd?

Someone brushes up against me. I nod politely as the guy takes his sweet time moving by. God, I'm getting old. There was a time when I wouldn't have noticed or cared about being in such close quarters.

Another guy passes by and looks me over before turning to whisper to his friend. I tug at my tie absently. Before I left, I changed into a nice suit in case the club had a dress code but clearly I shouldn't have bothered. The people in this club are wearing everything from leather and chains to body paint.

Also, they all look about fifteen years old.

I lean over to Ethan. "Maybe I shouldn't have worn a suit. They probably think I'm here to audit the place."

Ethan says something but I don't hear it because my

eyes just locked on a girl dancing on top of a speaker. My feet move in that direction until I'm standing below her. Her dark hair whirls around her face as she gyrates. She's wearing a black thong. I only know that because this angle gives me a direct line of sight up her dress.

Me and the guy right next to me. He's wearing a shirt so tight it looks like he might Hulk smash right out of it at any second. He's also wearing a baseball hat. Indoors. I roll my eyes.

"Stop looking up her skirt, asshole!"

Ethan appears at my elbow. "How did I know this was how the night was going to end?"

The guy glares at me before moving away slightly. He's still directly below Anya.

"*I said—*"

Ethan steps between us. "Do you really want to start a fight?"

"*Yes.*"

The way Anya is dancing has tequila written all over it. She's drunk and there is no way in hell I'm walking away without making sure she's okay.

"*Anya!*"

When I yell her name, she pauses her gyrations. A goofy smile spreads over her face when she sees me.

"Law! I'm dancing!"

The guy looking up her skirt isn't pleased that I've gotten her attention. "That's my date!"

I point at Anya. "Not anymore. Get lost. The free show is over."

He looks like he's about to say something else but when Ethan crosses his arms, his shoulders sag. He moves away.

"Okay, Anya. It's time to come down."

She shakes her head. "We're on a date! I'm supposed to be having fun."

I move forward quickly, alarmed at how she's swaying. After a bit more cajoling, she finally crawls to the edge of the speaker and then half rolls over the side.

"Shit. Hold on, baby."

With Ethan's help, we manage to get her down without breaking anything but not until after she flashes the entire club.

Ethan slams his eyes closed and turns his face in the other direction. "*I didn't see anything.*"

Anya slaps my arm. "I'm allowed to have fun for once."

"Yeah this is a barrel of laughs."

She loses her footing and I have to bend over to keep her from hitting the floor. Before I can straighten someone grabs my ass. I look over my shoulder to see a guy walking by. He winks.

"Did I forget to mention *Spectrum* is a gay club?" Ethan yells.

"Yes. You did."

Suddenly his questions about whether I'd been here before make a lot more sense.

He smiles. "This was worth coming out for."

"You know what, I'm not even mad. I look damn good in this suit."

"I'll take your word for it."

## *fourteen*

ANYA

HE'S MAD, I can tell.

Law doesn't talk the whole way home. But he doesn't have to. I know his mad face. His eyes crinkle at the corners and his dark eyes flash. It's actually the hottest thing ever. Then I remember that he basically crashed my date and demanded I leave with him.

Who the hell does he think he is?

"You shouldn't have come. I was having fun."

The lie is bitter on my tongue. The date was a bust from the moment we met outside the club. Clint definitely wasn't the shy guy he'd claimed to be. He started drinking heavily as soon as we arrived and had no concept of personal space. After pushing his hands off my ass one too many times, I'd eventually climbed up on the speaker just to get away from him.

Putting on a show for the crowd wasn't what I'd planned for the night but at least up there I could dance in peace.

As if he can guess my thoughts, Law makes a low humming sound. "Really? You were having fun with the guy who was staring up your skirt like a sex offender?"

Somehow I manage to stop the smile tugging at my lips. Law would never be accused of subtlety. Whatever he thinks comes straight out of his mouth. That straightforward bulldozer approach can be a problem at times but I can't deny I miss it.

Not that I want him to know that. He's already sure I'm going to come crawling back to him. The last thing I will ever admit is the undeniable flash of happiness I'd felt when I looked down and saw him in the club.

"I'm not sure what looking at my ass has to do with being a sex offender. He's a guy. I have a great ass. He's not the only one who was looking."

"Believe me, I am well aware of that."

The crinkles around his eyes get deeper. I have to resist the urge to reach over and smooth them out. It's instinctive, this desire to make him happy and soothe him when he's upset.

How long will it take before I don't care anymore?

The thought makes me so tired.

It's been a long time since I went out drinking and

clearly I don't have the tolerance for it anymore. All the dancing and sweating has left me feeling vaguely nauseated. I close my eyes. I just need a moment to rest before I finish telling Law to go to hell.

The next time I open my eyes, I'm snuggled into my favorite position in Law's bed. He always said he didn't care which side he slept on so I took the side closest to the bathroom. My pillow is bunched under my arm and I have a leg thrown out of the covers. It's dark but my eyes adjust quickly and I make out Law next to me. He's fully dressed and on top of the covers.

It hurts looking at him so close but so untouchable. Everything I want is right there but I can't have it.

He turns his head but doesn't open his eyes. "You're supposed to be asleep."

Busted, I bury my face in my pillow. "Why am I here? You said you were taking me home."

"I wasn't sure how much you had to drink. This way I could make sure you stayed on your side and didn't vomit in your sleep."

Shame makes my voice very small. "You didn't have to do that."

"Yes, I did. Good ole' Law. Always does the right thing."

"What does that mean?"

"Nothing. Just thinking about something Thomas said earlier."

"How is he? How are Jo and the kids?"

Thinking about his brother's family makes me smile. They're so different but Tommy loves his brother unreasonably. That doesn't stop him from giving Law a hard time whenever he possibly can. Watching those two snark at each other is always entertaining.

"Same as usual. He did make sure to tell me I'm a jackass before yelling at one of the kids and hanging up on me."

Maybe I'm just drunk but this strikes me as hilarious and I bury my face in the pillow to cover my snickers.

"You're laughing, I can tell." He sounds grumpy but I can hear the smile in his voice. "He likes you better than me, anyway. Just one more reason for him to tell me I'm a dumbass now."

The reminder that we are, in fact, not together stops my laughter. Then I'm just sad. If things had ended differently, Thomas and Joelle would have been family.

"He worries about you."

"He doesn't need to do that."

"He idolizes you."

Law grunts. "He definitely shouldn't do that."

"Why not? He told me you basically saved him by taking him in so he could finish high school."

Before he even speaks, I can feel his agitation. "He still has a big mouth. Apparently his kids aren't keeping him busy enough if he has time to talk about ancient history."

He rolls over to face the other direction and it feels like the temperature in the room plunges twenty degrees. It's funny how you can feel so alone even when another person is right beside you.

"All I ever wanted was to know you," I whisper.

He doesn't answer but his side of the bed is eerily still. Maybe this is just one more thing that's going to wedge us apart but drunk Anya doesn't care. Instead, I feel emboldened speaking into this dark room. Law is the one who chased off my date and drove me home like I'm some errant teenager who snuck out with a boy. The least he can do is hear what I have to say.

"You would never let me know you." This time I say it louder, my fury rising the longer he ignores me. "I want to understand where you come from. What makes you who you are."

With a little huff, he rolls over to face me. Now that my eyes have adjusted, I can make out his features since we're so close.

"That isn't who I am. That's more about my father than about me."

I want to argue but something tells me to wait. After a few minutes, his hand traces over the comforter between us until it's close enough to touch.

"We used to hide from my father together. Tommy is five years younger which doesn't make much difference now but was huge when I was ten and he was five."

His finger stops right next to my arm. I hold my breath waiting to see what he'll do next. When he edges closer, the warmth of his hand next to mine is so jarring that I almost jump.

"We had this chair that was just big enough for both of us to fit behind. I'm lucky I was such a skinny kid. It was always about something stupid. He would scream at my mother about where she'd been during the day and what she was wearing. And we would just hide and hope he didn't notice us."

My heart hurts and the sound of my throat as I swallow seems so loud that I worry he'll hear it. I don't want to do anything to distract him even though listening is agony.

"When I got older I started to intervene. He wouldn't ever hit hard enough to leave bruises, he was too smart for that. He was a corporate lawyer but he knew enough about criminal law to keep from leaving any evidence behind."

"What about your mom? Did she ever try to get help?"

He sighed. "She divorced him and left. He got full custody of us. All the years she'd been in therapy and on anti-depressants to deal with his bullshit worked against her in court. He made her look unstable and like it was in our best interest to stay with him. It was just one more way for him to hurt her. He didn't even want us. She lives with her sister in New Mexico now. We see her at Christmas."

"I'm sorry, Law."

He cleared his throat. "It was a long time ago. I graduated and got the hell out of there as soon as I could. I got a scholarship to Columbia and moved to New York. Worked my ass off in college and then got a job at a big agency in the city. I never planned to come back."

"What happened?"

"Joelle got pregnant."

I had known there was a large age gap between the children but I hadn't done the math before. Now I realized that they hadn't just been young when they had their oldest son but they must have been teenagers.

"They were still in high school."

He nods. "My father was furious when he found out. He already had one son who was a disappointment going into marketing instead of law. All his hopes were on Thomas to attend his alma mater and then eventually join the family firm. That's actually how I know Ethan. His father is a partner in a law practice with my father and uncle back home."

"Wow. I didn't realize you two went that far back."

"Yeah, he's a good guy. He has been there for me since the beginning. He witnessed my father chewing me out once so he knew that he wasn't the charming, affable good guy he pretended to be."

"Well, I know Thomas didn't go into the family business so I'm sure your father wasn't happy about that."

"No, he threw him out. He wanted Tommy to convince Jo to have an abortion. He didn't care what they wanted. All that mattered was that it would look bad to have a son who was a teen parent with his high school girlfriend whose family was from the wrong part of town."

"Bastard," I whispered.

He laughed. "He is a bastard. When Tommy called, I wasn't sure what to do. My job was in New York and that wasn't going to help him since he wanted to stay near Jo so they could eventually get married. Then one of the partners at the firm I worked for called in a favor and got me a job in finance at a friend's firm in DC. I moved here and did marketing freelance in the evenings. Tommy lived with me for two years and finished high school. We were close enough to Chesapeake that he could go visit her on the weekends."

"Chesapeake?"

"It's in the southern part of the state. That's where I'm from. Anyway, after they were married they lived with Jo's parents while they went to college so they could help with my nephew. Now my brother teaches Virginia State history to high schoolers."

A small sigh escapes at this little tidbit. How is it possible that over the past two years I never knew he was from Virginia? When I'd asked where he was from he'd always said DC.

"So you took Tommy in, helped him finish high school and made it possible for him to stay close to the love of his life? I understand why he said you saved him."

Law is quiet for a moment then the hand that was touching mine pulls back.

"No, I abandoned him for years. I only came back when there was no other option."

All at once, I wish that Law had just taken me home. Spending time with him like this is so dangerous. Because it hurts so much to see the difference between how others view him and how he views himself. He doesn't see the good that he does and only focuses on the bad.

But I see all of him, every complicated layer, and I wish he could see it. If I could I would draw a portrait and hang it on the wall so he could see the beautifully flawed, strong, stubborn, loyal man that I see.

In the dark of night, snuggled up next to the only man I've ever truly loved, it would be so easy to say *screw it* and just stay with Law indefinitely. Years would pass with us living, working and playing together, doing everything on Law's timetable and the way he wants.

If this is how he felt married to Elizabeth, then I

understand why he thinks marriage is toxic. Losing your identity to love someone else is the worst thing I can imagine. It's the ultimate betrayal of self.

"It was all a long time ago. It doesn't matter anymore."

My soft sigh floats between us. He reaches over and squeezes my hand.

"Go to sleep, baby. We'll figure it all out in the morning."

———

WHEN I WAKE UP, the events of the prior night are the first thing on my mind. Normally after something happens, I torture myself with all the *would-have, could-have, should-haves*, but today I don't even bother replaying the crappy date.

The headache currently pounding behind my right eye is punishment enough.

A quick glance to the side shows that Law has already gotten up. He's always been an early riser. My phone is propped on the nightstand next to me beside a bottle of aspirin and a glass of water. Law knows how alcohol affects me.

Suddenly I remember the date Ariana accepted for this morning. I'm supposed to be having coffee with someone.

I pull the pillow over my face to cover my groan. The

last thing I want is to drag my hungover body out of bed to meet some guy at a coffee shop. But I'm not a quitter so I'll see this through. It's not enough to just claim to want a new life. I have to be willing to put myself out there and see what other guys have to offer.

*But these guys aren't really interested in you, are they? They just want a hook up and pretty much any woman they find attractive will fit the bill.*

They aren't going to hold me if I wake up with a nightmare or listen to me bitch about a bad day.

*Law did those things,* I think mournfully.

But he won't give me the one thing I need. Assurance. A promise that he'll be there forever.

Instantly, I shake off the negative thoughts. This is not how I want to approach dating. Of course I won't find anyone great if I immediately assume the guys will be creeps. I check my GlowUp message. *Drew* is probably a perfectly nice guy.

If I want something different, I can't keep doing the same thing.

Which means I have to get up and get going.

After a quick pit stop in the bathroom, I walk out to the kitchen. The coffeemaker is still warm and the television is on in the living room.

Where is Law?

I check the garage, my stomach sinking when I step down into the empty space. He left.

Strangely let down, I call an Uber. While I wait, I take a quick shower and throw on one of the oversized college shirts I used to wear to sleep in and a pair of yoga pants. Looking down at the stuff in the bottom drawer of Law's dresser, *my drawer,* I realize it's probably time I clean it out and bring this stuff back to my apartment.

My phone vibrates. My Uber is waiting outside so I slam the drawer closed. I'll figure that out later. Preferably when I'm not hungover and late.

There's no time for me to go home so I'm heading straight for the coffee shop. It's in Logan Circle which is a pretty trendy part of DC. I'm trying not to read too much into this guy's choice of coffee shop. Maybe it's just close to his place. It doesn't necessarily mean he's a hipster.

When I arrive, I recognize him from his profile picture immediately because he's wearing the same shirt. It's red with a huge picture of a wolf on it. He's already drinking a cup of coffee so I go through the line and get a blueberry muffin and a latte. At least that will give me something to do if we don't hit it off.

Five minutes later, I stop next to his table. He looks up from the book he's reading and then stands so fast his chair falls over. The woman sitting at the next table gives him a dirty look.

"You must be Drew." I stick out my hand, hoping to avoid the social pressure to hug hello.

I've never really understood that one. Hugging someone you've just met is the height of weird but it's suddenly a thing. Refusing only makes you seem standoffish so I've been subjected to more stranger hugs in recent years than I'm really comfortable with.

"I am. Drew, I mean." He sticks out his hand and then proceeds to shake mine vigorously.

Before he can make any other sudden moves, I sit at the table. He takes his seat again, pushing aside his book.

"What are you reading? Anything interesting?"

He flips it over. "Nothing. Just a graphic novel."

My eyes land on the picture of a middle-aged man on the back cover. He's wearing a suit and looks pretty serious. Not that older men can't write graphic novels but the author photo on the back looks like someone who is about to give a lecture about calculus.

"Graphic novels are cool. I like true crime novels and mysteries."

Why does conversation feel so forced? I look around frantically, hoping to come up with something else we can talk about. A barista behind the counter yells out a name and someone walks up to the counter.

"Nice coffee shop. I've never been here before."

I figure that's as innocent a conversation topic as can be

found. Now that I've served the ball, it's up to him to return it.

"Yeah, I like this place. I come here during the week a lot to work on my screenplay. *Achoo!*" He covers his face with the crook of his elbow. "Sorry. Allergies."

"Oh it's fine. I get allergies, too. So you're writing a screenplay? That's exciting. What's it about?"

That was way too enthusiastic but hopefully if he's talking about himself it won't feel like I'm dragging conversation out of him word by word.

"It's about a guy who puts his heart and soul into loving a woman."

*Okay.*

"That sounds–"

"He gives her everything and then she just rips his heart out. After that he's a broken shell of a man. A living corpse walking around the city looking for a reason to exist. It's a zombie movie."

*Of course it is.*

His eyes search mine and I take a huge bite out of my blueberry muffin.

"Mmm. Mmm hmm."

Apparently that passes as understanding because he launches into a long description of the plot. I nod every few sentences and try to look alive. I was already hungover this morning but this date is making my head hurt worse than the tequila.

"*Achoo!* Anyway, the long road is symbolism for the journey I had to take to get over the breakup. I mean the journey *he* had to take. The character, I mean."

"Right."

His arm has moved off the book on the table and I can see the spine now. The title is *Get Over Your Ex Already*.

I sigh.

Ariana owes me big for this one. After the fiasco with "Shy Clint" last night, my patience for nonsense is set to zero. At least I got a blueberry muffin out of the deal. Once I take some more pain medication and my head doesn't feel like it's about to split open, I'll be able to enjoy it.

"So this has been great but I really have to go."

He pauses mid-sentence. "You do? But we haven't had a chance to talk about our compatibility yet. Our goals."

"My only goal today is to not have a hangover anymore."

Also to eat my weight in ice cream. Not that anyone else needs to know about that part.

"Okay. But maybe you could call me sometime? I'd love to... *Achoo!*"

He tries to cover his mouth but doesn't make it. I watch in silence as the full spray of his sneeze covers my hand.

And my blueberry muffin.

He sniffles. "So I guess that's a no on getting your phone number?"

LAW

AS I APPROACH the door to Anya's apartment, I shake off the nerves bouncing around my stomach. They've been there ever since I got back from my grocery store run to discover she'd already left.

I wasn't disappointed exactly but more surprised. She's never been a morning person so I'd anticipated coming back to find her still warm and rumpled, waiting for me. We could have had breakfast together and talked. Either way, I'm here now and hoping that a breakfast burrito from her favorite deli will entice her to let me in.

Going out this morning was a critical mistake. If I'm going to show Anya that we need to get back together, I should have kept her on my turf. Her apartment is an unknown. I've only been here a few times over the past two years, mainly to drop her off when her car was in the shop or so she could pick up something she needed before we headed back to my place.

After knocking I stand back to make sure she can see me in the peephole. When she opens the door, her face betrays her surprise.

"What are you doing here?"

Before she can think about it too much, I sweep past her and into the living room. The television is on and there's a movie playing. Her shoes are kicked off carelessly next to the couch.

"I brought you a breakfast burrito."

Her eyes narrow on the bag in my hand. "How did you know I was hungry?"

"You're always hungry."

I place the food on the small coffee table in front of the couch. Then I hold up the other bag I'm carrying.

"Also you forgot your dress at my house. I figured you might want it."

Anya takes the small bag containing her dress from my hand with a grateful smile. "Thank you. Considering it's not even mine, I definitely need it back."

"You left this morning before I could apologize."

"For what? Law, I'm the one who should apologize. I ended up taking over your bed."

"Still, I was sorry to see that you were gone."

Her eyes drop. "Yeah, I had somewhere else to be."

The silence becomes uncomfortable as I realize what she means. She had another date. Jealously spreads through my veins in a rush of heat.

While I was out buying eggs to make her breakfast, she was rushing off to meet some other guy. I clamp my lips together, not trusting myself not to ruin the moment with angry words.

Like it or not, Anya has the right to date whoever she wants. I'm not here to contest that. My goal is to show her that dating someone else is useless when we both know they won't compare to what we already have. Our connection is undeniable and she'll never get this by swiping left and right on random dudes.

"So anyway, thanks for bringing this by." She walks toward the door.

Annoyed by her sudden desire to kick me to the curb, I sit on the couch and get comfortable.

"Did you hear that we lost the Sayer account?"

"Yeah, I heard Mya talking about it the other day. That sucks."

Curious now, I arch an eyebrow. There's no way that's all she overheard.

"I'm not telling you anything," she mutters.

Chuckling, I slip my leather jacket off and toss it over the back of the couch. After sitting back down, I stretch my legs and wait. She may not want to tell me but her conscience will win in the end.

No matter what is happening between us personally, Anya would never withhold information that could help me in business. It's just not who she is.

Finally she sighs. "Mya thought that was why Elizabeth was calling you. That she was trying to rub it in your face or whatever."

"Great. So it was Sunfire that got the account then?"

"Yes. Sorry."

The pity in her eyes makes me feel like I'm on fire. That's not what I want no matter what happens.

Is it ridiculous and humiliating that my ex-wife keeps stealing accounts from right under my nose?

Of course.

But I don't need anyone's pity.

What I need is strategy.

"I've been thinking we could target some of their competitors. Maybe I'll put a team together just to work on outreach campaigns to potential clients. If we show them examples of the kind of advertising we could create on their behalf, it might bring in some new business. What do you think?"

Anya's still hovering by the front door. "Sounds good. Maybe we can talk about it at the office on Monday."

"Trying to kick me out already?"

Her glare shouldn't be as amusing as it is. She's adorable when she's mad. It hits me in that moment just how much I've missed this. Not that I don't have other friends. Ethan has been my rock on many occasions and we're bonded over our mutual hatred of our fathers.

However, the relationship I have with Anya is unlike any other in my life. There are things I would never say to Ethan, not because he isn't trustworthy but just because it would be too weird.

Even between friends there are lines you don't cross. Things you don't say.

With Anya every line is blurred and I'm as comfortable with her as I am with myself. There's nothing I can't say. A little stunned by that insight, I rub my suddenly damp hands on my jeans.

"I don't want to leave," I finally admit.

Her eyes soften a bit before she looks away. When she speaks again, her voice isn't quite as sure. "We shouldn't be spending time together outside of work."

"This is work."

"How is this work?" she asks with a soft chuckle.

"Your contract says *other duties as assigned.*" My reasoning might be thin but I'm willing to stretch that far.

"Hanging out with you is an *other duty?*"

"No, but business planning is. We've lost some accounts over the past year and we need to replace that revenue. I have to decide what accounts we should compete for."

Apparently Anya gives up on getting rid of me because she plops down on the couch instead. She unwraps the breakfast burrito and takes a huge bite. Her hum of pleasure makes me smile.

"Don't look so smug. I'm just a sucker for a good burrito."

"I didn't say anything."

We sit in silence for a bit as she enjoys her food.

"You know, it's none of my business..." She pauses and glances over at me. Something about the hesitant look on her face makes me nervous.

"Just say it. I wouldn't have asked if I didn't really want your opinion."

"You aren't the only person who can make these decisions. Why can't you delegate some of this? You have an amazing team. Mya can read people like a book. Milo could sell ice to a polar bear and Kevin slides right in there as the goofy, friendly guy and by the time people figure out he's directing them it's too late. You have to trust the people around you at some point. Otherwise, why are they there?"

She takes the last bite of her burrito and then crushes up the foil. Meanwhile, my mind turns her words over.

Am I that bad at asking for help?

Does my team feel like I don't trust them?

"You're tired, Law."

I'm not sure if she means that literally or figuratively but in either case, it's true. At least it sounds like she cares which gives me hope.

"Hold tight. I know what you need."

I lean back against the couch cushions, relaxing for the first time since I found her gone this morning. She didn't want to let me in but she did.

Maybe that's progress.

———

WHEN I WAKE UP, Anya is gone. I'm stretched out on her couch with my feet hanging off the end. Groggy, I sit up trying to figure out how long I've been asleep.

"You're awake." Anya appears at the end of the couch.

She's changed clothes into leggings and a loose shirt. The tight points of her nipples are clearly visible through the material. There is no way she's wearing a bra. Everything clenches and I glance away hoping she doesn't notice my instant erection.

"How long have I been asleep?"

"Only an hour. I didn't want to wake you. I figured you needed the sleep. Especially after babysitting me last night."

She sits on the couch, our legs brushing together intimately. Several tendrils of hair have escaped the hasty ponytail she scraped together at the back of her head. Those tendrils kiss her neck, tempting me to follow them with my lips.

When she turns to say something else, she pauses. Something on my face must give away my thoughts because she bites her lip.

"We can't."

"I know."

But even as I say the words my hands reach for her hair against my will. Tunneling through the glossy black strands until I can cup the back of her head with my hand.

The sound that escapes her throat is guttural, a primal call for dominance. It speaks to the deepest part of me, the part that has always reveled in the intense connection we have. My fingers curl into a fist, pulling her hair securely as my lips find her throat. She must have showered because her skin is still slightly damp.

I drag my tongue up her neck until I reach her ear. "Are you still going to ask me to leave?"

She slaps her hands against my chest and for a second I think she's pushing me away. Then the sharp points of her nails dig into my skin.

"Law, please. Just touch me."

Never one to let a lady down, I lift her into my lap easily until she's straddling me. Her legs wrap around my waist as our mouths collide, helping her grind against my lap. She pulls back only to tug the loose T-shirt over her head. My lids fall to half-mast when her perky little nipples come into view.

I knew she wasn't wearing a bra.

Looking deep into my eyes, she takes one of my hands and brings it to her breast. Groaning, I massage and pinch the sensitive tip until she's gasping my name with each stroke. Turning us until we're splayed across the couch, I lean down and take one of the tight tips in my mouth, sucking and biting so hard it has to hurt.

There's something frantic about touching her now, everything inside of me screaming to touch, taste, hold and caress her before the opportunity is taken away.

Being underneath me doesn't take away Anya's ability to drive me crazy. If anything she takes it as a challenge, canting her hips upward to provide maximum friction. All coherent thought is gone as she drags her pussy back and forth over my erection.

It's the kind of grinding that would *definitely* turn into fucking if our clothes evaporated.

How can she think she'd find this with someone else? Nothing has ever felt this good.

Those guys she's going out with just want one thing. They're willing to say whatever they need to in order to get her out of her clothes. I'm the only one looking out for her.

*Is that what you're doing?*

My conscience pricks at me. Just because Anya falls apart whenever I touch her doesn't mean this is really what she wants.

Am I really so different from those other assholes?

Maybe they're saying what they think will get them in her pants but I'm doing what I *know* will get me there. She's been clear about what she wants from me and instead of respecting that, I'm using my knowledge of her body to make her temporarily forget.

"Wait. Anya, we have to stop."

She whines, her lips continuing their exploration of my neck. Her hips don't stop moving until my hands land on her ass and hold her in place.

"Nooo. Why are we stopping?"

The lust in her eyes almost breaks my resolve. Then she bites my lip and the sting of pain makes me groan.

*Why the hell am I stopping this again?*

"This isn't what you want," I remind her. "And I won't be like those other guys who just do things to get you in bed."

My words break the spell because she pulls back and pushes her hands through her hair.

"You're right."

I climb off the sofa and turn to face the other direction so she can put her shirt back on. There's a picture on the wall of a meadow with flowers in it. It looks way too generic to be something Anya would pick out. There must be a story behind it. Staring at the unfamiliar landscape only drives home how rare it was for us to spend time at her apartment.

Considering that her place is in the city, it actually would have been convenient to spend some of our weekdays here to save us the drive out to the suburbs.

Why didn't we ever do that?

We always spent time at my house. Everything was on my turf. Everything was for my comfort. It never occurred to me how selfish that was which makes me feel even worse.

How did I spend two years with Anya and never ask what she preferred?

"Was I a bad boyfriend?"

"You weren't my boyfriend."

"Anya, I'm being serious."

When I turn around, she is sitting on the couch staring out the window. She doesn't look at me but her foot tapping against the carpet gives away her agitation.

"No, you weren't a bad boyfriend. I never would have loved you if you were."

"Past tense?"

Immediately, I regret the question.

Anya walks to the front door and opens it, waiting. The warmth we generated has left behind a distinct chill. It's something I need to get used to, being apart from her. This is going to be our new normal. I no longer have the right to touch her whenever I want and I'm not the one she'll confide in when she has a secret.

The thought makes me unbelievably sad.

Even though this is what Anya wants, the thought of her feeling like she can't talk to me makes me ill.

What if she needs something?

When she doesn't say anything else, I grab my coat from the back of the couch and shrug into it. I walk to where she's standing, still avoiding my eyes. Without considering the wisdom of my actions, I take her arm gently. She tenses but still doesn't look at me.

"I'm going now but I just wanted," I clear my throat, unsure of exactly what it is I'm trying to say.

After this I'll be keeping my distance so it suddenly seems even more important that I get this right.

"What is it, Law?" She looks at me finally, her eyes searching mine for something I can't give.

"I just wanted to say that no matter what happens, I will always care about you. If you need me, I'm there. Any time. I hate to think of you stuck in a situation like yesterday with no one to call."

She nods slowly as tears appear in her eyes. Just like always, she sees beyond the words to my true meaning.

"You really want me to call you when I'm out on a date with someone else?"

Pulling her forward, I press a kiss to her forehead. "I

want you to call me whenever you want to. For whatever reason."

A tear finally breaks free and rolls down her cheek. She flicks it away angrily. She still isn't looking at me and I know I need to get out of there before I forget all the reasons I stopped us on the couch.

I'm walking down the hallway when she calls my name. I turn back to see her leaning against the doorframe.

"Eventually, I *will* find someone else. You need to be ready for that. And so do I."

*sixteen*

ANYA

THERE ARE some things that only an impromptu Girl's Night can fix. Clearly I'm not doing such a great job untangling the great Law mystery on my own. So Ariana and I are hanging out at one of my favorite bars.

It started out as my favorite because it was close to the office and cheap. Now it's my favorite because Jessi bartends here and makes me killer drinks whenever I've had a crappy day.

Jessi leans over the bar to shake Ariana's hand. "It's great to finally meet you. Anya has told me a lot about you."

Ari glances over at me. "She's told me about you, too."

Jessi laughs. "You don't have to dance around it. Yes, I'm the girl who felt up your friend's husband back in the day. It's weird, I know."

I grimace, forgetting that I'd told Ari that story.

Granted, it was a long time ago and *way* before Mya and Milo got together. But still, I didn't mean to put Jessi on the spot.

*Awkward.*

"Sorry. I forget sometimes how small our world really is."

Jessi starts making my usual drink. "It's all water under the bridge now. That was before Mark figured out that he can't live without me."

Her fiancé must feel his ears burning because he looks down the bar to where we're sitting. He winks at Jessi. He's a big hulking guy that towers over her petite frame.

"How did you convince Mark to take a chance? He used to be so grumpy."

Jessi shrugs, a private smile on her lips betraying how happy she is with said grumpy guy.

"You can't make a man realize what's good for him. You can show him what he's missing by living your life. Either he'll get on board or he'll miss out."

Ariana takes another slurp from her drink. "I like her."

"Me too." I look over my shoulder and then almost fall off my barstool. "Oh my god. Casey!"

She flings her arms around me in a crushing hug. I'm so overwhelmed that for a moment my head spins. We worked together side by side for a while before we started hanging out as friends. I'm so used to having her around that I didn't realize how much it threw me off my game once she left.

"What are you doing here? Aren't you supposed to be on your honeymoon?"

"I still am on my honeymoon." She smiles prettily.

Ari wolf whistles. "She used to be so sweet and innocent. What happened?"

Casey sticks out her tongue. "I'm still sweet. But Andre likes me a little dirty, too."

With that declaration, Jessi slides her usual drink across the bar. "This is on the house. For the newlywed."

Casey takes it gratefully. "Thanks, Jessi. Anyway, we decided to come back because my mom had an accident at work. She's totally fine but I wanted to check on her for myself. We decided to continue our trip a little later closer to Christmas. Andre wants to show me how Italy does the holidays."

"That's so romantic. Plus, it means we get to have you here for a little longer."

Ariana makes a rude noise.

Casey elbows her. "You missed me."

"No, I didn't."

Casey laughs and rests her head on Ari's shoulder. "I love you too, crazy lady."

Jessi leans over the bar. "This is perfect timing. We need a third opinion since Anya won't listen to us."

Betrayed, I put both my middle fingers up. Jessi loves that, grinning widely as she goes to serve another customer a few seats away.

"Tell her the whole story," she yells over her shoulder.

"What did I miss?" Casey asks.

I sigh. "Okay, it all started at your wedding."

A half an hour later I've caught Casey up on everything that happened after my near death experience with one of her wedding cupcakes. She listens intently to the whole thing with only a side glance for Ari when I mention our pact and then wide eyes when I talk about hiding in the closet at the GlowUp party.

She especially seems to enjoy hearing about my disastrous dates with "Shy Clint" and "Drew Sneezy".

"All that happened? How long was I gone?" Casey says.

Ari looks at me.

"What?"

"You left a few things out."

"I didn't leave anything out."

"Sex on the desk with the boss-ex."

I groan. "Oh yeah. That happened."

Ari clears her throat. "And yesterday's sex with the boss-ex."

Casey gasps. "Yesterday?"

"Okay yesterday wasn't sex. It was just hot making out

on the couch." I'm not sure why it matters so much to keep the details clear but it feels like my hill to die on.

"Desk sex and hot making out doesn't sound like you've broken up," Casey points out.

Busted, I drop my head to my arms. "Maybe I just need a sign from the universe. I'm so confused. I'm sure Law is too since I'm definitely giving him mixed signals."

Ari gives me side-eye. "Girl, the fact that your legs fall open every time you see him is not a mixed signal. That's a pretty clear green light to me."

"Okay, so I need a sign telling me how to stop greenlighting sex with my ex. Is that better? Besides, I did *not* sleep with him yesterday."

"You wanted to."

Caught, I take another gulp of my drink.

Ariana laughs. "Got her."

"I still can't believe you met Seth Barrington," Casey says. "Andre wanted him to invest in something, I think. But he's known for being really picky. Andre says he's brilliant."

"It's no big deal. A mega mogul like that probably meets a million girls every day. I doubt he would even recognize me if I fell in his lap."

My phone chimes.

Casey looks around. "What's that?"

Ari perks up immediately. "I know that sound. Is that a GlowUp match?"

I pick up my phone and tap the notification. The app opens showing my newest match. I double tap it to view the profile. The username is *sbinthecloset*. I blink twice at the name. They both lean over my shoulder to see my phone screen.

"Is that who I think it is?" Ari asks.

There are only two pictures. One is of a dark haired man from behind. He's wearing a suit and looking out a tall window. The other is of a closet filled with coats.

Casey's mouth falls open. "Wait. SB as in..."

"Oh snap. It's. About. To. Go. Down," Ari chuckles.

A squeal comes out of Casey that almost shatters my eardrum. "This is so exciting! He definitely remembers you. *A picture of coats.* Clearly he's sending you a message."

"Let's not get too excited. He can't exactly put his real picture on here."

Casey makes a face. "Ariana, deal with her."

Ari lets out an aggrieved sigh. "You asked for a signal. Well." She gestures to my phone. "LEFT TURN BITCH!"

While they crack up laughing, my thumb hovers over Seth's profile photo.

Even though I'm downplaying it, my pulse picks up speed as I stare at the picture of coats.

This isn't like the other dates I accepted. Seth is on a different level. He's not a drunk guy with wandering hands or an over-histamined screenwriter with a vendetta. If I accept this match, it feels like taking a permanent step away from Law and toward a new future.

Then I remember Law walking away from me. Walking away for the last time. That kiss on the forehead was a kiss goodbye and we both knew it.

"Okay universe, I get it."

I take a deep breath and then click the Accept button.

———

IF I THOUGHT that Seth would be waiting around for me to accept his match, then I quickly get a wakeup call. He doesn't respond until almost midnight. I'm in bed with a cup of hot tea on the nightstand next to me. The GlowUp notification startles me so badly I fumble my ereader and drop it over the side of the bed.

"Note to self. Tell Mya they need to change the default sound on the app."

I'm sure any normal person could change it but I've always been annoyingly terrible with technology. It's probably not worth the energy it would take for me to figure out how to do it.

His message is short and to the point.

SBINTHECLOSET

Hidden in any closets lately?

Not the most original opening but it still makes me laugh. I can't imagine that Seth Barrington has hidden in many closets, ever.

ANYAPETROVA

Not lately. But there's always tomorrow.

SBINTHECLOSET

Let's save the closet for another time. I'd rather see you in the light of day. Meet me for dinner?

I'm not sure if it's just the format but he comes across as the perfect mix of solicitous and commanding. Still, I'm not sure I'm ready for a formal date yet. Who knows the type of place he'd take me. The idea of putting on a fancy dress to dine on snails and caviar, or whatever it is that billionaires eat, is incredibly intimidating.

ANYAPETROVA

I can do lunch tomorrow. There's a cute little place near my office. Does that work?

SBINTHECLOSET

For you, I'll make it work. See you then.

A coffee shop close to the office feels like more my speed. Before I can chicken out, I send him the address. There's a chance the chemistry we had at the party was a fluke. A quick coffee date is perfect since I only have an hour for my lunch break. It's a built-in eject button.

After drinking my tea, I read for a little while before cutting off the light. Our coffee date may not be a big deal but that doesn't stop me from feeling guilty.

———

THE NEXT MORNING FLIES BY. Not in a good way. I overslept and then had to shower, dress and eat breakfast in less than twenty minutes. Then the supplies I ordered for the office arrived except somehow everything was duplicated. Now I have a room filled with boxes of extra supplies and no idea what to do with all of it.

By the time lunch arrives, I feel like a rag that's been hung up wet.

Sharon waves as I pass the reception desk. I told her earlier I would be leaving early for a lunch date. On the way out, I stop in the bathroom and try to fix my frazzled appearance with a little makeup. Lipgloss and highlighter make me feel a little more normal.

The coffee shop I recommended is this adorable little place called *Cuppa*. By the time I arrive, Seth has already claimed a table near the door. He stands as I approach.

Suddenly nervous in a way I wasn't before, I cross my arms and then uncross them.

How is it possible that he's even more handsome wearing sweatpants?

It's obvious he's going for an unassuming vibe today and looks more like a frat boy who just came from the gym.

"Hi."

"Hey. I'm glad you came." His dark eyes are as intense as ever as he yanks out the other chair for me.

Grateful for something to do, I sink down into it. I've been here so often that I don't need the menu but I pick it up anyway. He takes his seat just as the waitress appears to take our orders. He orders a black coffee and a scone.

"I'll have a vanilla latte and a blueberry muffin." Then I get a sudden mental image of the fate of my last blueberry muffin.

I'm still haunted by it's sad dive into the trashcan.

"*Wait.* Scratch the blueberry muffin. I'll have a scone, also. Thanks."

The waitress takes the menus with a huge smile for Seth. "I'll bring your orders right out."

As she's walking away, Seth raises his eyebrows.

"Sorry. Blueberry muffins bring up bad memories for me now."

"Everything with you is a story."

The way he says it is so affectionate that I relax a bit. His dark hair is flopping all over the place and he has at least a day's worth of stubble on his face. He's just a guy, right? There's no reason to be nervous around him. Yes, he's handsome and accomplished and basically every girl's fantasy. But he's also the same guy who would rather hide in a closet than socialize.

"So... sbinthecloset?"

He laughs. "It got your attention, didn't it?"

"That it did. I was shocked to see you have a profile on the app."

"I didn't. After we parted ways I regretted not asking for your number. We didn't really exchange any personal information and I wasn't sure how to find you. Then it occurred to me that I knew one thing about you."

"That I was using GlowUp."

"Exactly. It turns out being one of the owners has its perks."

"Hmm, so you shamelessly hacked the app to find me."

"I did. I'm pretty sure the head programmer wanted to quit after dealing with me."

The waitress reappears then with our order and only then do I realize we're both leaning over the table to get closer. After she leaves, I take a nervous sip of my coffee. We sit in silence for a few moments before we both start talking at once.

"I was–"

"What do–"

That breaks the ice and we both laugh. He holds out his hand indicating that I should go first.

"This is embarrassing but I don't actually understand

what you do for a living. All I know is that everyone says it's really impressive."

His eyes sparkle with amusement. "I worked on Wall Street for years then I started investing for myself. Now I enjoy funding new businesses that have potential."

"That's really cool. Everyone seems excited about GlowUp."

"I hope so. But tell me more about you."

He listens attentively as I describe what I do as an office manager. Then we talk about our families. I'm not surprised to learn that he is the oldest of three.

"Do I seem like the bossy type?"

I raise an eyebrow. "We both know the answer to that question."

"My little sister is actually the boss of all of us. She has me and my brother Dane wrapped pretty tight."

The image of him trailing after a pigtailed girl makes me smile.

A warm feeling spreads through me as I sip my coffee. This isn't what I was expecting at all. Talking to him feels so comfortable.

Seth takes a huge bite of his scone. "What are you thinking about over there?"

"Nothing."

"Don't get quiet on me now. You told me you like to choke on meat the first time we met."

My chest trembles with laughter. "Pretty sure that's not what I said."

"That's what I heard," he insists.

"It's really nothing. Just, I have a confession."

"Should I be worried?" For the first time since I arrived, he looks wary.

"That sentence sounds way more ominous than it actually is, I promise."

He exhales heavily. "I hope so. You have no idea the kind of stuff people say to me. One woman I dated turned out to be a corporate spy who'd been assigned to get close to me. Then there was the limo driver who pretended to have cancer so I'd donate to his GoFundMe. I've had five paternity lawsuits from women that I've never even met."

"Wow. It's nothing like that. I just didn't expect to like you so much."

He places a hand over his chest and makes an exaggerated shocked face. "You didn't?"

"No. I was expecting someone spoiled and entitled. Not someone I can actually talk to."

His eyes stay on mine. "I knew we would have fun."

"How could you tell? Did my scintillating closet conversation seduce you?"

"Your closet conversation was refreshing."

The bustle of the coffee shop gets louder as more people file in. When I check the time on my phone, I'm legitimately sad to see that I only have about ten minutes left before I need to leave.

Seth nods to my phone. "You need to get back?"

"Soon, unfortunately. And I really mean that. I'm having fun."

The smile that stretches across his face makes him look years younger. My initial impression of him, as someone jaded who carries a heavy weight on his shoulders, was correct.

Based on some of the random things he's said (five paternity lawsuits?) I can tell he expects the worst from people. I get the impression that he doesn't smile like this often.

"Would you like to have dinner sometime?"

"Dinner?"

"Yes. Us at a nice place eating a meal that takes a long time to consume." He hangs his head. "I'm completely messing this up. I want to take you on a date."

"We're on a date."

He scoffs. "This is not a date. Coffee is not a date."

"It is so!"

"I have a sister. I know how these things work. Coffee is the date you make when you need an easy escape in case the guy is a serial killer."

"I don't think coffee would protect me. Besides the jury is still out on the serial killer thing."

"There are no bodies in my backyard. I promise."

"You have a backyard?"

He raises his eyebrows.

"Oh *right*. I forgot."

I wouldn't have thought it possible but his gaze warms even more.

"You forgot that I'm rich. See what I mean? Refreshing."

He's so open with his feelings, something I'm not used to with men. I need to be honest with him, also. Despite the fact that Law never wanted to call himself my boyfriend, I love him.

*Loved* him.

I shift uncomfortably, determined to make it "past tense" as Law had asked.

Either way I'm not sure if I'm ready to try again. Strange as it may seem, I feel a little protective over Seth. I don't want anyone to hurt him.

Not even me.

"I just got out of a relationship. Other than two traumatizing first dates, this would be the first time I've dated anyone else. I just thought you should know that."

He nods. "That's fair. However, I would still like to take you to dinner."

"I'll think about it."

"Now it's my turn to make a confession. I can be pretty persistent when I want something. Just fair warning."

# *seventeen*

## LAW

"STILL WITH ME, BOSS?" Mya asks.

I sit up straighter. "Yes. Where are we on the Bite Me Bakery account?"

After a long day, it's torture to sit through a bunch of status updates but it's a necessary evil. Keeping abreast of what projects we have in the pipeline allows me to ensure there are no surprises down the line that might lead to missed deadlines and angry clients.

The headache pounding at the back of my head has nothing to do with overhearing Anya saying she was leaving early for a lunch date.

Nothing at all.

"Okay, what is going on with you lately?"

"What?" Surprised at her tone, I stare at Mya in surprise.

Despite being boss and employee, we've always had a friendly relationship. All of my team leads are amazing but Mya in particular has been a crucial part of building the Mirage Agency into the powerhouse it is today. That's the main reason I made her a VP.

Not only that but I *like* her. She's fun and generous and always willing to go the extra mile for a fellow employee or a client.

Right now the face that's usually smiling is set into a distinct frown.

"With all due respect, we might as well not even bother with these status updates since you haven't heard a single thing I've said. The LA office could have burned down for all the attention you're giving this meeting." Mya places her notes on the chair next to her.

"Sorry."

She gets up and then closes my office door. "Talk to me, James. I would like to think we're friends by now. I just want to help."

"Nobody can help."

Mya bites her lip. "Is the agency in trouble?"

"No. Why would you ask that?"

"People talk. It isn't just us noticing that Sunfire keeps stealing accounts from us."

"Great."

"This isn't just a job for me. I love this place and I don't want to work anywhere else. Milo feels the same way. If Elizabeth is going to fight dirty, then maybe we should, too."

Before I can talk myself out of it, I spill the whole story about the cabaret club and all of my fears about taking on another risqué client. Mya listens closely, only interrupting once to clarify a point. She paces back and forth as she takes it all in.

"I understand your fears. It's always a risk to step outside the lines but maybe that's exactly what we need."

"What if it blows up in my face like last time?"

"Unless you plan on running away with one of the cabaret dancers, I think that might have been a once in a lifetime thing."

Her wry comment breaks the tension and we both laugh. For the first time, I think there might be light at the end of the tunnel. My worries about the business crashing down around me have been heavy on my mind for the past few months. I'm so used to doing everything on my own and that includes shouldering the burden of worry.

But as Anya pointed out, my staff members are capable and ready to help out.

The only one holding them back is me.

"You're right. I've been so focused on the negatives but there are a lot of things we could do with this account to take us to the next level."

Mya nods her agreement. "It's a risk but I think it'll be worth it. Let's make a pros and cons list. There might be some things we haven't considered that will help make the decision easier."

When things get quiet, I look up to find Mya watching me.

"What?"

"Ever since Elizabeth called, you've been different. I just want to say that sometimes things go tits up."

"Excuse me?" I splutter with laughter at the mental imagery that phrase calls to mind.

Mya shrugs. "That's probably not the most professional way to put it but it's true. Sometimes in life things just don't go our way. Even if we do everything right. *Especially* when we do everything right."

Her words hit a chord inside. Isn't that often how I've felt? Years of playing by the rules and walking the straight and narrow and look how things turned out.

"Yeah. I hear you."

"Anyway, my point is that the potential for disaster is always there but that doesn't mean there's something wrong with you. It just means you haven't found what does work for you. *Yet.*"

An hour later, we've come up with an impressive list of reasons for and against bringing on the cabaret club. We also generated a list of research topics the junior agents can tackle for us to make the decision easier. Just before she leaves, I call out her name. She pauses next to the door, her eyebrows raised in inquiry.

"What do you do? When things go... tits up."

Her soft laugh makes the question less awkward.

"Personally, when it feels like nothing makes sense, I go where I feel safe. Where things seem right."

---

MYA'S WORDS are still on my mind hours later. I'm thinking about what she said even as I approve the month's payroll and field a call from an angry client about the late notice our accounting department sent.

As I'm dealing with all the usual annoyances of being the boss, I'm turning her words over and over in my mind.

Where do I feel safe?

It's not something I've ever really thought about before. It's not like I'm a little kid anymore, hiding with my brother from one of my father's tirades. No one controls me and I'm strong enough to defend myself. I don't need other's opinions or approval.

But even as I have the thought, I know that's not what Mya meant. She wasn't talking about physical safety, clearly.

When I look up, I'm standing outside of Anya's office.

Resigned, I knock once and then wait. When she doesn't answer, I twist the doorknob and walk in.

"What in the hell?"

I peer around the room in confusion. Every inch of floor space is covered with boxes. The label on the closest one is from the company that handles our office supplies. I recognize the name from the large invoices that come across my desk quarterly. We used to order supplies monthly as needed but Anya worked out agreements with our suppliers to get us better discounts if we made larger orders.

I wonder if she's working on some special project and needed to order way more supplies.

"Oh. Law. I guess you've seen, huh?"

I turn to find Anya standing behind me wringing her hands.

"Special project?" I gesture to the boxes.

She huffs out a sigh. "No. I think I made a mistake. My usual order must have been doubled somehow. I'm really–"

Before she can even finish the sentence, I reach over and take her hand. "None of that. If you made a mistake, it's no big deal. We'll just store these until later. We can ask accounting to check on it for us. The mistake might be on the other end."

"You're not mad?"

"Anya. Of course I'm not mad."

She shrugs. "I just thought... it's whatever."

"You thought that I'd be mad at you just because you left work for a date?" I grit my teeth, frustrated that I said what I was thinking.

"No, it wasn't because of that."

"So you *were* on a date?" I give up any pretense that I'm not interested. That ship has clearly sailed.

"It was no big deal. Seth just wanted to meet for coffee."

At the sound of his name, I'm slammed with the memory of the two of them laughing in that stupid closet like schoolgirls. Then his hand on the small of her back as they'd left together. Clearly he isn't giving up.

"Right. No big deal."

She turns to her desk and hits a key to wake the computer up. "Anyway, I'll get these boxes taken out of here by the weekend."

I pull my phone out of my pocket and send an email. Five minutes later, Wallace, Kevin and Milo appear in the hallway.

"Where do you want 'em, boss?" Wallace rolls up his sleeves.

"Anya, did you already get what you needed from the boxes?"

She looks at me in shock. "Yes, I put all the stuff I need to distribute in this box right here. But you guys don't have to carry them. I can do it."

I turn back to the men waiting in the hallway. "Take them to the empty storage room for now."

The men move quickly, each grabbing a box and heading out. I take one as well. When I get back to her office, the guys are already carrying their second boxes back down the hallway.

Anya leans against the doorjamb. "I was going to huff and puff and blow smoke about how I could carry them but I won't. That was a lot. Thank you."

"You're welcome."

She brushes a stray hair away from her forehead. "Um, did you need something? I mean, was there a reason you came looking for me earlier?"

Now it's my turn to shrug. "No, I just figured I'd check in. See how things were going."

She nods slowly. "Okay. Well, thanks."

I continue down the hall toward my own office. When I get there, I stand in the middle of the room feeling lighter than when I left even if I'm now covered in dust and slightly winded from lugging that box.

If I hadn't gone down there, Anya would have tried to carry all those boxes by herself. It bothers me that she thought I'd be angry with her over a simple mistake. Anya knows me. She knows I would never treat any of my employees that way but *especially* not her.

All I've ever wanted was for her to be happy.

As happy as she makes me.

My ass lands in my desk chair with a thud. I wipe my face with a shaky hand.

Because I suddenly know *exactly* what Mya meant.

———

THE NEXT TWO days feel like two years. All I want is to get through the weekend. The GlowUp official launch event looms before me like a spectre.

Mya's team has been running full speed ahead preparing for the gala. I still can't believe they pulled it off but then again when you have pockets as deep as Seth Barrington, you can do whatever you want.

Even plan a black-tie event in the nation's capital with only two weeks of lead time.

The thought of Seth Barrington makes me scowl. I don't know if Anya has seen him again since their coffee date but my money is on yes. Barrington is known for being like a dog with a bone when he's after something.

Now Anya is the bone.

I slam the lid of my laptop.

"Are the numbers not playing nice?"

When I look up, Elizabeth is leaning against the doorjamb. She chuckles at my shock.

"You were always in your own little world when you

were working on something. I used to think a bomb could go off and you wouldn't even notice."

"What are you doing here?"

"I wanted to see you." She says it as if it should be obvious. As if she didn't have to get on a plane and fly two thousand miles to make this little rendezvous happen.

"I see you're still the Queen of Understatement. How did you know I would even be here?"

"Once a workaholic always a workaholic. Good Ole' James. Some things never change." She runs a finger over the nameplate on my desk.

"Where's Gareth?"

Liz looks at me with those gray eyes that used to fucking slay me. "I left him. I told you what I want."

It's suddenly a million degrees in the room and I tug at my tie. Hearing that she wants me back was one thing on the phone and another thing entirely when she's standing right in front of me.

It would be poetic if she looked terrible after our five years apart. A unibrow or a sudden wart on the end of her nose would feel justified. Except she looks the same as always with long blond hair and the artful spray of freckles on the bridge of her nose that I used to find so charming.

"You can't just show up here after all this time and think that nothing has changed."

"I know that. But still, we were married for ten years. All that history, James. No one ever knew me like you do."

"Knowing you didn't seem to matter much in the end."

Abruptly, I stand. I carelessly toss my laptop into my messenger bag. I have to get out of here.

Elizabeth moves back as I continue gathering things off the desk, trying my best to ignore her.

"If I could go back, I would change so many things. Especially the part where I hurt you. I am so sorry."

Seeing her like this has thrown me off my game. I'm so used to hating her that I can't handle hearing her say she's sorry.

"You didn't deserve that. All you ever did was love me," she whispers.

Then she wraps her arms around my shoulders and presses her lips against mine.

# eighteen

ANYA

YOU KNOW how when you tell yourself not to think about something, it's suddenly all you can think about?

Dinner with Seth has been on my mind for the past few days. Before we parted ways at the coffee shop we exchanged numbers and as he warned me, he's persistent. He asks me out everyday and manages to make it funny instead of annoying.

The first night he texted asking what I was doing. Since I'd just seen him that afternoon I hadn't expected to hear from him so soon.

SETH BARRINGTON

What are you doing?

ANYA PETROVA

Just sitting around.

SETH BARRINGTON

Me too. Want to sit around together?

SETH BARRINGTON

While people bring us food?

ANYA PETROVA

LOL nice try.

His next attempts were no less entertaining. I was at work dealing with a glitch in the calendar program that mixed up everyone's appointments. After turning it over to tech support, I'd been on the verge of locking myself in the bathroom for the rest of the day when his text came through.

SETH BARRINGTON

I'm having a bit of an emergency here.

ANYA PETROVA

R U OK?

SETH BARRINGTON

My refrigerator is broken. What do I do?

ANYA PETROVA

Did you call for a repair?

SETH BARRINGTON

I already did. But maybe you could bring me some food while I wait?

SETH BARRINGTON

Then you could stay. And eat it next to me
:)

ANYA PETROVA

Oh, you're good.

In between the creative attempts at getting me to agree to another date, he sends me funny stuff he sees while out and about in the city and even a picture of him with his little sister. Every single thing contributes to the overall picture of a brilliant, misunderstood and slightly lonely overachiever.

If this is how he operates in the business world I'm starting to understand why he's so successful.

Things with him are so easy. I could just say yes and I have a feeling he would make sure I'd never want for anything again.

Plus he's not exactly hard on the eyes.

What a choice. The emotionally scarred older man who has nothing but bad experiences with love or the optimistic billionaire who wants the same things I do?

The oddest part is that I can't even talk about it with anyone. It feels wrong to ask Casey and Mya to take sides since they know Law, too. Jessi has been so tired lately working all night and planning her wedding. Truthfully, we've grown apart due to having opposite schedules. Really, Law was my closest friend and I was used to telling him everything.

But what's to say that Seth couldn't become my next best friend if I gave him the chance?

Decisions. Decisions.

Almost like he can hear my thoughts, a text from Seth pops up on my phone.

SETH BARRINGTON

Dinner tonight?

My fingers hover over the screen. Finally I put my phone away and get back to prepping the salad. It's so tempting to just say yes and spend a pleasant night being distracted by the sexy, intense man who is actually interested in spending time with me. But then I have a sudden mental image of Law sprawled on my couch sleeping.

How long can I pretend that I'm ready to move on? It's become painfully obvious that dating isn't going to be as simple as just finding a new guy. I need to think about this and not make any rash decisions.

"What are you doing to those cucumbers?"

My mom's voice breaks my concentration and I look down to see that instead of chopping I've been mushing the same few pieces of cucumber into pulp.

"Oh, sorry. I guess I'm a little distracted."

My mom smiles knowingly. "How is James doing? Working late tonight?"

I smile weakly and shrug. It was way too complicated to explain to my mother so I kind of just neglected to tell her that we broke up. Maybe it was time to come clean but honestly she'd called because Pop was having a good day. I wanted to spend time with them and enjoy the moment while it lasted. My mom deserves to enjoy this break. I don't want to give her something else to worry about.

"Yeah. We have a new account at work. Things have been really busy."

"Maybe soon you can take a little time off. Drag that handsome man here for dinner. He works too much. Your father was the same way." She clucks disapprovingly.

Even though she has said something similar many times before, it strikes me differently today. Like most, I don't really think about my parents as a couple. They've always been just Mom and Pop. But they dated and married young, right in the middle of my father's demanding education and later, his demanding career.

Did my mother ever feel the way I do? Like she was just an afterthought?

"Mom, how did you know Pop was the one? Did you ever have doubts?"

Her eyebrows raise slightly. "Of course. Everyone has doubts sometimes. Your father's passion for his work was part of why I loved him. But it's hard to compete with, also."

It makes me feel a little better. Clearly she found a way to work through whatever fears she had since they've been married so long.

"How did you deal with that? I mean, did you ever think about giving up? Maybe finding someone else?"

The timer on the oven goes off and she wraps her hand

with a dishtowel before reaching in to pull out a pan of hot rolls. After that she carefully slathers the tops with butter.

"This may surprise you but yes, I did."

I sit at the counter, resting my chin on my fist. As many stories as she's told me over the years, I've never heard anything about another boyfriend.

"What happened? Did you guys break up?"

She shakes her head. "There was another gentleman interested in taking me out but I eventually turned him down. It wasn't the first time I'd had another man show interest but it got your father's attention because this man was a friend of ours. He was educated and very handsome. All the girls thought so."

"Pop knew about this other man?"

"Of course. I told him. We have never kept secrets. If you can't be honest and talk to each other then you shouldn't be together anyway."

"Wow. So, Pop got jealous, huh?"

"I think he was jealous for a little while. Then he realized that he was the one I loved. He was the one who held my heart. I will admit that having a little competition helped him move things along faster." She glances over her shoulder and winks.

"What would you have done if Pop didn't want to get married?" I pick at the edge of my nail, not wanting to see her face when I ask the question.

"That is a difficult question. Things were different then. People got married. It was what everyone did. I can't pretend to understand how young people do things these days." She comes to stand next to me at the counter and puts a soft hand against my cheek.

"But any man who doesn't know how lucky he is to have you isn't worthy. You are a gem, my sweet girl."

"Thanks, Mom."

Somehow she seems to understand that I need a little space, so she bustles around the kitchen getting the rest of the food together. I should help but instead I sit at the counter thinking about the unanswered text on my phone.

My mom's story didn't give me any real answers. Just because my father got jealous and realized he couldn't live without my mother doesn't mean I can expect that outcome.

But the one thing that sticks out is the communication.

Law and I have done a lot of talking *at* each other instead of talking *with* each other. Maybe if we can set our differences aside, we can come up with something we both can live with. My parents definitely will be a little disappointed if I never get married but after today, I honestly think my mother would understand.

Pop held her heart.

Law holds mine.

My heart clearly only has one space and Law is squarely in the center of it. Is it fair for me to go on a date with Seth or any other guy when I'm thinking about someone else? Aren't you supposed to close one chapter before starting another?

I need to talk to Law.

"Mom, I can't stay for dinner. I'm sorry."

I put my phone in my handbag. It's Thursday night so Law is probably still at the office. He usually stays late on Thursdays and Fridays to wrap everything up so he won't need to work weekends. Hopefully, no one else will be around and we can talk privately.

"Go find him, Anya. That man loves you. I'm sure together you can figure things out. Make him hear you because every minute you have together counts. Every single minute."

Tears sting my eyes as she pulls me into a gentle hug. The fact that she understands without me having to tell her makes it easier somehow.

"Let me just say goodbye to Pop before I go."

She brushes away a stray tear from my cheek with her thumb. "Please let me know how you are later tonight. No matter how old you get, I still worry about my baby."

"I will. I promise."

Pop is sitting at the dining room table, reading a newspaper. Mom bought him an ereader but he still likes to hold a physical paper in his hands. Earlier when I came in, he gave me a kiss and asked how work was going. It was unexpected since it's been a long time since he's remembered anything about my job. Then we played a few hands of his favorite card game, *Durak*.

He beat me every time, as usual.

When he hears me approach, he lifts his head and smiles. "There you are. Dinner must be ready."

"Almost but I can't stay. I wanted to say goodbye before I left." I lean over and kiss his cheek.

He reaches up for my hand and then squeezes several times. It's something he used to do when I was a little girl. At church when I was bored and fidgeting, three squeezes. When my best friend in middle school suddenly didn't want to be my friend anymore because she got a boyfriend, five squeezes. When I graduated from high school with a 4.0 GPA, more squeezes than I could count.

"I understand. You don't want to stay here with the old folks. I guess that means your mother gets me all to herself." He laughs at his own joke.

My heart lifts seeing him in such a good mood. So much of our interaction recently has been about what's wrong. Doctors, diagnoses and all the things he can no longer do. Today we could just live. For just a little while, we have him back.

"I'll come back in a few days. We can play cards again."

Just when I reach the door, I hear him call my name. When I look over my shoulder, Pop gives me a stern look.

"Don't forget your curfew is ten o'clock, young lady."

My heart sinks but I manage to keep the smile on my face. My mom gives me a knowing look from the doorway to the kitchen.

*Every minute counts.*

*Every. Single. Minute.*

"Of course. I love you, Pop."

"Love you, too."

His eyes go back to his newspaper and I leave, ignoring the heavy feeling in my chest.

———

WHEN I PULL into the parking garage at the Mirage offices, I take a deep breath. Law's car is still parked in his assigned space. On the drive, I'd convinced myself he wouldn't be here and the conversation could wait until tomorrow. Now there's no excuse.

I take the elevator up and then step into the empty reception area. There are still a few other people here because I can hear someone talking in the distance and then the distinct sound of the microwave beeping in the break room.

"Hey, Anya." Milo pauses in the doorway to his office. "Didn't I see you leave earlier?"

I flash a smile as I walk by. "I can't stay away!"

Law's office door is partially open so I poke my head in. I don't want to disturb him if he's in a meeting.

All I see is the back of a woman's blond head as she kisses him. Even though I can't see her face, my memory supplies the visual of gray eyes, freckles and an annoyingly perfect nose. I'd recognize Law's ex-wife anywhere after how many times I've google-stalked her.

There's nothing more I need to see here.

As I walk back down the hall, I keep my head down so no one will see the tears on my cheeks. I hit the button for the elevator and luckily it opens immediately. As the doors close, I pull out my phone.

ANYA PETROVA

I would love to have dinner. I'm starving.

SETH BARRINGTON

We can do Les Printemps if it's not too pretentious for you.

ANYA PETROVA

That's perfect. I'll meet you there.

When the elevator opens on the parking level, I stride to my car, purpose in my steps. Fine dining with a handsome billionaire shouldn't feel like a consolation prize.

CALL it muscle memory or maybe just good old-fashioned shock but my body doesn't immediately recognize the panic signals my brain is sending out. Movement at the door finally breaks the paralysis and my hands land on her shoulders and push until there is a foot of space between us.

"What the hell are you doing?"

Liz pouts. "Don't be like that. We're so good together. You can't deny it." She's still reaching for me, trying to get closer.

I feel vaguely sick to my stomach.

The door to my office is slightly open. I walk out into the hallway and look both ways.

Was there someone here?

I hate the idea of any of my employees seeing me kissing Liz. Considering all the shit she's put us through, she'd better hope Mya doesn't catch her in here. My tie feels like it's strangling my neck and my blood is rushing fast. I'm not sure why I'm so concerned about being seen but I feel an urgency to check the whole building. Speeding up, I enter the reception area, looking both ways.

Milo is next to the elevator holding a bag of popcorn in his hand. He pops a handful in his mouth but pauses mid-chew when he sees me appear probably looking like a madman.

"Everything okay, boss?"

"Yeah, I just thought I saw someone. You weren't at my door a few seconds ago, were you?"

He shakes his head. "Might have been Mya. She was working late, too."

"Okay. Yeah, it was probably her." I rub the center of my chest with the palm of my hand. My heart throbs one more time, so hard it feels like some kind of heart attack.

By the time I get back to my office, I'm surprised to see Liz still standing in the middle of the room.

*"You're still here?"*

Annoyance tightens her lips to a flat line. "Yes, I'm still here. Are we going to talk about this?"

"It's over between us. It has been for a long time. I have a great life here and there's someone..."

I'm not sure how to describe whatever is going on with Anya. My insistence on not putting a label on it seems a bit ridiculous now, especially since it's clear that what I feel for her *is* something. If it wasn't, I wouldn't feel so terrible about Liz kissing me. It's not technically wrong but it *felt* wrong.

There's only one woman I want to kiss.

"There's someone." I decide to leave it at that.

Liz shrugs but her nonchalant posture seems forced. "Okay. But just be careful. Your girlfriend isn't as loyal as she seems."

"*Right*. Because I'm going to take relationship advice from you."

"I'm just saying, one of my employees is still friends with her." She doesn't say anything else but purses her lips.

My first thought is an immediate denial. There is no way. Anya isn't like that. But how many times have I wondered how Liz's agency was able to compete for so many of the same clients? They always undercut our bids as well. I'd assumed it was a side effect of Liz and I working together for so long. She knows how I think and as she always says, I'm pretty predictable.

It honestly never occurred to me that she might have inside help. Anya may not even realize that the gossip she's sharing with her friend could be used against us.

"Even if that's true, why would you tell me?"

"Because I feel bad and it's time we wipe the slate clean."

"I have to go."

She says something else but I don't hear it as I grab my stuff and leave. My mind is a jumble as past loyalties war with new experiences and the only thing I know for sure is that I'd rather be anywhere but here.

———

ANYWHERE but here turns out to be my car in the parking garage. The noise in my head started to subside once I was on the elevator. By the time I got in my car I was breathing easier. Being around Liz is like having my mental battery slowly drained.

That woman is a vampire.

Before I can second-guess myself, I pull my phone out and call my brother. When he answers, I don't even bother with hello.

"How did you know you could trust Joelle?"

The only reason I can tell I've shocked him is the momentary pause before he answers.

"What brought this on?"

In the quickest summary ever, I tell him what happened with Liz. His long extended groan brings a smile to my face.

"I hate that you're questioning everything now based on that she-beast."

"I'm not. Let's just say it's something I've been thinking about lately."

He sighs. "I don't know if I believe that. This isn't like you. We never talk about this stuff."

"I thought you were crazy, did you know that?" I interrupt. "When you told me you were going to marry Jo."

"Of course I knew. I was seventeen with a pregnant girlfriend I was determined to marry. I thought I was crazy, too. But you took me in anyway when Dad threw me out. You helped me finish high school."

"You told Anya I saved you. You give me way too much credit."

"No, I don't. You were a jackass and you still are. But you did save me. I deal with facts. That's what happened."

"Maybe I just didn't want to be like him," I mutter finally.

He's quiet for a while and I wonder if he's running through the same memories I am. Not being like our father is one of the only goals we share. We're very different people, my brother and I, but on that point we completely agree.

As if he can hear my thoughts, Tommy sighs. "That's a good enough reason in my book."

"Everything here is fucked. I thought I was doing the right thing letting Anya go. Now Liz shows up and all I can think is that I refuse to go backward. So where does that leave me?"

"Look, I wish I had some easy answers for you. You know we love Anya but that doesn't mean she's the right one if the two of you don't want the same things. But I knew I could trust Jo the same way I know I can trust you. It's like I always tell my students. History tells the story. You showed up for me every time I needed you."

"Anyone would have done that."

"No, they wouldn't have. You could barely afford food for yourself but it was never even a question for you. You just do what needs to be done. Jo stood up to her parents for me. She's proven herself. That's the best way to decide who is trustworthy. Look at their actions."

After hanging up, I text Anya.

JAMES LAWSON

We need to talk.

As soon as I hit *Send* I wish I could take it back. *We need to talk* is universal shorthand for bad news. Technically the news *is* bad, Liz showing up is a disaster of apocalyptic proportions, but I don't want Anya to think I'm mad at her or something.

JAMES LAWSON

Something happened today and I wanted to talk to you about it. Can I come by?

That's when I realize she might not even be at home. It's Thursday night which means being at home for a boring old dude like me. But Anya is young and beautiful. She's probably on another date right now.

My fingers clench around my phone.

JAMES LAWSON

> If you're already out maybe I could meet you after? I could buy you a cup of coffee.

Now it sounds like I'm asking her on a date. I'm practically begging for a date with my not-ex-girlfriend. Frustrated, I toss my phone on the passenger seat. Sending any more texts will be borderline stalker status.

Maybe I should drive by her apartment. She's probably ignoring my texts, not that I blame her. But maybe she'll take pity on me and open the door if I'm actually there. As soon as I make the decision, I change my mind. It's not fair to show up at her place when I don't know what I'm doing or how I'm feeling.

This isn't her problem.

It's my problem.

Resigned to another lonely night, I pull out of the garage and drive slowly through the dark streets of the city. DC has a vibrant nightlife so things are busy even at ten o'clock on a Thursday night. Just as I take the turn onto 23$^{\text{rd}}$ Street to head out of the city, my phone rings. I never pick up when

I'm driving so I ignore it. A minute later, a notification dings for a voicemail. I pick up the phone and use voice commands so it will play the message out loud.

*Hello? This is Marta Petrova. You left your phone number on the card when you sent flowers for my birthday. I'm so sorry to bother you James but I can't reach Anya. Her father—*

There is a muffled noise, like she's covering the phone and talking to someone else.

*If Anya is with you please tell her that her father had an accident this evening. We're at the hospital now. GW. Thank you.*

Before the message even ends, I'm already pulling a U-turn in the middle of the road. A horn blares behind me but I ignore it and pray no cops witnessed that maneuver.

Speeding back in the other direction I run through my memories of today. Anya was in the office like usual and left around five o'clock. She hadn't said anything about going out after work but who knows if she had plans. Maybe she's out with friends or on another date.

I grab my phone and then use voice commands to call Anya. When it goes immediately to voicemail I realize she must have turned it off.

Or it ran out of power.

Either way she's out there somewhere and has no idea

that her father is in the hospital. I debate going to her place and checking if she's there but then I make a snap decision.

At the next light, I take the turn toward George Washington University Hospital.

# twenty

ANYA

BY THE TIME I arrive at the restaurant, I'm numb. Actually I'm not even sure how I got here. The entire ride is a blur. All I keep seeing is the back of her head and her arms around his neck.

Did that really just happen? Law was kissing his ex-wife?

He hates her.

"Reservation?"

I look up to find the hostess staring down her nose at me. She's tall and thin with the type of figure I could only achieve if I ate nothing but salad and ice cubes.

"I'm meeting Seth Barrington here."

With those few words, I apparently move up the ladder of importance in her mind because she instantly drops the attitude.

"Oh, of course. Mr. Barrington has already arrived. Follow me."

She leaves the front podium and I follow dutifully, wishing that I'd thought to go home and change first. When I went to my parents' for dinner this evening, I went straight from work so I have on plain blue slacks and a gray blouse. My shoes are low-heeled and I feel about as plain as paper compared to everyone else in here.

Holding my head high, I focus on the hostess's back as we move through the dimly lit restaurant. It's hard to believe this is the same place where the GlowUp beta launch party was roughly two weeks ago.

So much has happened since then. I almost wish I could time travel back and warn that optimistic Anya to run while she could.

"Here we are." The hostess gestures to a table tucked into the back. Seth is already seated but he stands when we arrive.

"Thank you, Sybil."

She preens. "Of course. Please let me know if there is anything else you require."

He holds my chair and I sit, grateful not to be on display anymore. I swipe a stray lock of hair off my forehead, trying not to feel so disheveled. Seth is back in what I imagine is his usual attire, a tailored suit that fits his athletic body perfectly.

Gone is the casual, guy-next-door who met me at the coffee shop. I look around the dim restaurant, at the crystal chandeliers and the elegant linen tablecloths. He looks like he belongs here.

Who am I kidding? He looks like he owns the place.

"I'm glad you could make it. Eating alone is so boring."

I smile gently. "I'm sure there are plenty of people who'd love to eat dinner with you."

He quirks an eyebrow. "None that won't ask me for money when it's over."

That surprises a genuine laugh out of me. He grins and leans back in his chair. Just like that the ice is broken and the same comfort we found at the coffee shop blankets the table.

"Don't take this the wrong way but I'm starting to wish we'd gone for takeout instead. This place is a little intimidating."

"We can ditch this popsicle stand and go get burgers if you want," he whispers conspiratorially.

I take a small sip from the water glass next to my plate. Even if the environment is a little stuffy, it's a beautiful restaurant and known for having fantastic food. I pick up the menu. They have crème brûlée.

Decision made.

"Well now that we're here, it wouldn't hurt to eat. Mya has raved about the desserts." My finger stops on the dinner menu. "Let's see what we have here. Veal Ragout. Beef bourguignon. Today's special is the coq au vin."

He snickers. "And she's talking about cock again."

My snort of laughter draws the attention of the diners around us and I press my hand to my lips trying to contain it.

"Don't make me laugh in this fancy place. They're going to throw me out."

Just then a waiter appears to refill our water glasses. "Monsieur Barrington. Are you ready for an *aperitif*?"

Seth clears his throat. "Actually I believe the lady is interested in today's special. Do you recommend it? I want to be sure it's good."

The waiter's spine stiffens. "We only serve the *best*, I assure you. Our chickens are organic and free range. Chef Rousseau earned his second Michelin star after perfecting this recipe and *Washington Gourmand* declared it the best on the east coast."

"Did you hear that, baby? It's the best cock in the city."

Of course that only sends us into another fit of laughter. The waiter watches with judgmental eyes, clearly insulted by our lack of decorum.

"I will return momentarily," he huffs, before flouncing off.

"Oh god, I'm going to need to leave a monster tip after this." Seth swipes a hand over his face before regarding me with amusement. "Have I mentioned I'm really glad you came?"

With a little sigh, I think about everything that happened earlier.

When I told Law that he had to be ready for the day when I moved on, I hadn't considered that the opposite was true, as well. Maybe his ex-wife can give him the non-committal type of relationship he desires. Or maybe he's just a single guy who is happy to have a one-night stand with an old flame.

Either way, it's none of my business.

The day I made the decision to move on from our not-relationship, two different forks in the road appeared. I'm on one path and now Law is on another.

"I'm glad I came, too. This is exactly what I needed." I pull my phone out of my purse and switch it off so I can give Seth my full attention.

It's time I take the first steps.

———

CONVERSATION FLOWS EASILY and after an hour, I forget why I was ever nervous in the first place. Despite his rarefied lifestyle, Seth is very down-to-earth and has endless questions about my childhood and what it was like growing up bilingual.

"I feel like I'm talking so much," I comment after I finish explaining the rules behind the card game I'd played with my father earlier. "I'm sure you don't care about Russian card games."

"No. Please, this is fascinating. I'm adopted so I've always wondered what it would be like to have that connection. Not that my parents aren't amazing. They are. But there's still a part of me that wonders, you know?"

"Yeah. I understand."

His eyes move over my shoulder and he suddenly breaks into a big smile. "I apologize in advance for whatever happens next. Also, don't believe anything he says about me."

A man stops next to our table and claps Seth on the shoulder. "He emerges! Good to see you out of your cave."

Seth hangs his head slightly. "Ignore him, Anya. That's what I do. This is Cooper Vane. Coop, this is Anya."

We shake hands and the instant our fingers touch, I have the urge to yank my hand back. Cooper raises my hand to his lips. There's nothing particularly weird about it but the interaction leaves me feeling slightly slimy. After he releases my hand, Cooper turns to Seth and smiles. It doesn't quite reach his eyes.

"I'll leave you kids to your dinner. Don't do anything I wouldn't do."

He moves on, joining a group at another table, but I can't stop watching him.

"Who was that?"

"One of my business partners."

My mouth falls open slightly. I'm not sure what I was expecting him to say but that wasn't it. The vibes coming off that guy were definitely not friendly, so to hear that they are supposedly on the same team is a little strange.

"You know him well?"

"I do. We've done a lot of projects together. He's one of my best friends."

"When he looked at you, I didn't get friend vibes. I hope I'm wrong but just be careful."

He puts his fork down. "I can't figure you out. You didn't respond to my text for so long that I assumed you were ignoring me. Now you're worried about me?"

My cheeks heat. He's being more direct than I expected but it's a valid question. With everything that's happened, he's been the recipient of plenty of mixed signals, also. Just one of the many things I regret about the past few weeks.

"Sorry about that. I wasn't ignoring you. I like you. You're one of the good ones. You deserve to get everything you're looking for."

"Why can't that be you?"

"Excuse me?"

"Why don't you tell me about him? The guy who is keeping me from having a chance with you."

"I'm sorry."

"Don't be. You feel things and you don't hide from your emotions. I could learn from that." He takes another bite of his chicken. "Will you attend the final GlowUp event with me? Even if I don't have a chance it'll be nice to have a friend to keep the bullseye off my back."

I take a small sip of my wine. "I would be honored to be your shield for the night."

"After this I'll take you home. I don't want to give you a chance to change your mind."

Smiling, I pull out my phone from my bag. "I won't. Sorry to be rude but I just need to text my mom so she knows I'm okay. I promised her I would. She worries."

"As moms do," Seth agrees. "Please feel free."

I turn my phone back on and as soon as it powers up, the screen fills with notifications.

"Whoa. What is going on? I have a bunch of phone calls and texts."

With mounting horror, I open my texts first. My mom left a bunch but my eyes immediately go to the last one sent by Law. It just says "IT'S ABOUT YOUR FATHER" in all caps.

"Is everything okay?" Seth asks.

"No. Something happened to my father."

Immediately he lifts his hand and when the waiter appears, he asks for the check. "Can you also have valet bring my car up? We have an emergency."

"Certainly, Monsieur."

"It's okay. You don't have to–"

Seth waves me off. "Of course I'll drive you. Just let me know where they took him."

Law's last message was clearly just to get my attention. The one right before it is longer and has all the information I really need. My father fell at home and was taken to the hospital. They admitted him and he included the room number. I text him back that I'm on my way.

"He's at George Washington."

"Let's go." Seth helps me up and I follow him to the front of the restaurant.

The valet holds the door open to the passenger side when he sees us coming. Seth slides into the driver's seat and speeds away from the curb. I'm so glad he's with me because if I was alone, I'm not sure I could handle driving safely.

"I guess I'll get my car later," I mumble. Not that it matters.

Why am I thinking about my stupid car?

A shiver wracks my frame and I rub my arms. Maybe I'm thinking about stupid stuff because it's easier than wondering whether Pop is okay.

"Don't even worry about that. I'll have my driver deliver it to your apartment. Text me your address."

Grateful to have something tangible to do, I pull out my phone and send him the message. When I next look up, we're pulling right in front of the ER entrance at George Washington.

"Thank you, Seth."

"You're welcome. Go make sure your father is okay. Don't worry about any of the rest of it."

With a grateful smile, I climb out of the car and walk into the emergency room. After asking the nurse at the front desk, I find the elevators and go up to the third floor. As soon as I step off the elevator, Law straightens up from where he was leaning against the wall.

"Where is he?"

Law holds out his arm for me to precede him and together we walk down the hall to room 307. Once we enter, I notice the bed is empty. My mom looks up and then lets out a soft cry.

"Anya! You're here."

I walk over and hug her. She's sitting so it's an awkward hug but I immediately feel better.

"What happened? Is Pop okay?"

She sniffs. "He's okay. They just took him for more tests since he was confused when they brought him in. He hurt his arm but it's not broken."

All the emotion that's been building since I first saw the flood of messages on my phone finally breaks.

I burst into tears.

Law grabs my hand and then my face is pressed against his chest. He rubs his hand up and down my back while I sob. Finally, I lift my head.

"Sorry. I just saw all those messages and didn't know what to think."

Mom puts a hand to her chest. "I only left for ten minutes to take a shower. Then I came out and the front door was open." She stops, shaking her head at the memory. "Anyway, I went looking for him. I didn't think to check the stairs at first. We never use the stairs."

"You couldn't have known he would leave the apartment, Mom. He's never done that before."

She nods but I can see that she still feels guilty.

"Well, I think I'm going to get some coffee. They said the tests would take at least an hour."

Law steps forward. "I can get that for you, Marta."

"No. I need the distraction. You two stay here and talk." She smiles slightly as she picks up her purse. If she's pushing us together it means she's feeling better.

After she leaves, I look over at Law. He's been so quiet I almost forgot he was still here.

Wait, why is he here?

"How did you end up here with my mom?"

He shrugs. "She had my phone number from the flowers I sent. She called me when she couldn't reach you."

"Oh. I guess that makes sense."

I close my eyes, wishing I could undo my decision to turn my phone off earlier. But just like I told my mom, there's no way I could have foreseen something like this happening. So there's no point stressing about it now.

"Thank you for leaving that message. It got my attention when I turned my phone back on. My mom had left so many it would have taken me longer to figure out what was going on and where I needed to be."

"Of course. Don't even mention it."

"You don't have to stay. I'm sure you have other things you need to be doing. Although I appreciate you staying with my mom so she wasn't alone."

"She needed someone here. So I'm here. And I'm not leaving until I know you're both okay."

My mom comes back with her coffee a few minutes later. Law gets a bottled water from the vending machine for me and checks some emails while we wait for my father to come back. An hour later, a doctor enters the room. He glances at us uncertainly before my mother tells him we're family.

The look on his face immediately scares me. I look over at Law. He takes my hand and squeezes it.

While the doctor discusses the test results, I try to listen but none of it makes much sense to me. Luckily Law is paying close attention and asks several questions. I'm grateful that he's here and I can tell by the worshipful expression on my mom's face, that she is, too.

He's such a good man.

Just not my man.

Not any longer.

# twenty-one
## LAW

IT'S ALMOST midnight by the time Anya's father is settled in his room and it takes us another hour to convince her mother to go home and get some rest. After we drop her off, I pull up to Anya's building. Her car is in her assigned space so I pull up right behind it blocking her in.

Anya climbs out of the car. She doesn't have a coat so I shrug out of mine and wrap it around her shoulders. I was expecting an argument but I think she's too tired to even question why I'm coming in.

When we open the door, Anya's roommate, Jessi, looks up in surprise. She's in the kitchen making a cup of tea.

"Hey! I thought you were in your room."

Anya hands me back my coat. "No. Pop fell earlier so we were at the hospital."

"Oh no. I'm so sorry. Is he okay?" Jessi abandons her mug on the counter and comes over to give Anya a hug.

"Yes. He'll be okay. It was just scary. What are you doing home?"

"Got off early. I have an exam tomorrow and I really need to study."

"I'm sure you'll rock it." A huge yawn interrupts her sentence. "Now I'm exhausted so I'm going to go to bed."

Jessi gives her another hug and then waves at me. "Me too. I need to get all the sleep I can before class tomorrow afternoon."

I follow Anya into her room and turn my back when she starts taking her clothes off. A few minutes later I chance a look and she's wearing pink pajamas. So far she hasn't protested me staying so I'm afraid to ask any questions.

She climbs into her bed. She looks so small buried in the midst of her huge comforter. As strong as she is, she's vulnerable, too. She deserves to be protected. I lean down and kiss her forehead.

"Thank you for bringing me home. I can always count on you."

"Good Ole' James." The bitterness in my voice is obvious.

"Are you okay?"

"Of course. It's nothing."

She's been through too much tonight as it is. The last thing I meant to do was make it about me.

"Come on. We've been talking about depressing stuff all night. I need a distraction."

"It really is nothing. Maybe I'm just tired of being quite so predictable."

"You're not predictable. You're steady."

"*Boring.* One of Liz's favorite words."

"Didn't stop you from kissing her," Anya mutters.

"That *was* you at the door!"

She rolls her eyes. "It doesn't matter."

"Why were you there?"

"No reason."

I seriously doubt she had no reason to be at my office door that late on a Thursday night. Especially when she'd already left the office for the day. My jaw clenches just thinking that Liz's stupid stunt cost me a chance to talk to Anya. Now the moment is lost.

"That wasn't what you think. Liz kissed me. I pushed her away."

"Does it matter? I can't be mad at you for moving on when I have, too."

The thought reminds me that I still don't know where she was before she came to the hospital. Clearly she didn't drive herself since her car was here when we arrived.

"I haven't moved anywhere. Liz claims she wants me back but she's just here to start trouble."

"What kind of trouble can she start?" When I don't respond, Anya chuckles. "I see. What did she say about me?"

I think for a moment about making something up but that's never been our thing. We never hid stuff from each other.

"She said the only reason they could steal clients is because her employee got info from you. Which I know is bullshit. You would never do that."

"But she made you wonder, didn't she? She's good."

"Anya, I don't believe her."

"I know but as long as she can mess with your head, she wins."

"I shouldn't have brought it up. You're exhausted. Take the day off."

All at once, all the events of the day hit me at once. I need to get out of here. Being near her when I can't hold her, kiss her and make love to her the way I want to feels like emotional torture.

"I'll let you get some sleep."

Her hand on top of the covers reaches over to touch mine. Then she turns my palm over and strokes down the center. My eyes fly to hers.

"Anya." It's both a warning and a plea. This is wrong, I

know it is, but I'm not sure how much self-control I'll have if she asks me for what we both want.

"We're both single. We can have sex."

Her blunt address should be off-putting but instead my dick rises instantly. He agrees with her.

"That's probably not a good idea."

"Isn't that what you wanted? Just sex. No strings. Well, that's all I'm asking for. I just want to feel alive. The way I always felt when you touched me."

My resolve is draining away rapidly, especially when she takes my hand and puts it beneath the covers. Her aim is spot on because she guides my palm down her pajama pants until my fingers slide right into a warm, wet paradise.

We both groan at the contact and Anya's back arches off the bed. The sight of her throat bared to me is too much to resist. I lean down and kiss her collarbone just as I curl two fingers and thrust deep.

"*Yes*. God, yes." Her tortured moan is not only a turn on but a huge ego boost.

She might be moving on but this is something only I can give her. Her body wouldn't be so starved if any of the other guys she was dating knew what the hell they were doing. She might not be mine but her pussy is and that's something. Hell, it's probably more than I deserve.

Maybe this is all I can give her but if so, I'll give her everything.

She owns my body. Every breath from my lungs. Every beat of my heart. It's all for her.

Her eyes open and lock on my face as she rides my fingers. She's getting close and all at once I want to be inside her when that happens.

When I stop, she groans softly until she realizes I'm pulling her pajama pants down. She lifts her hips to help me and then scrambles to pull her top off. I'm just as frantic, tearing through the buttons on my dress shirt before shoving my slacks and underwear down. She throws the comforter out of the way so there's room for me to get in the bed. I climb on top of her, both of us sighing with pleasure the moment we meet skin to skin.

For a brief moment, I wonder if I'll embarrass myself and come before I even get inside her. But after a few deep breaths, some of the blood goes back to my brain. It hits me then, the thing we've forgotten. Anya has always been on the pill but that doesn't mean we don't need protection, especially since she's been dating.

"Do we need a condom?"

Anya looks up at me and bites her lip. "No. I haven't been with anyone else."

Joy coupled with shock rushes through my veins and I lower my head to kiss her. When our lips meet, heat blooms and I reach down to guide myself to the one place I always want to be. She lets out a long sigh of pleasure as I slide home. My lips cover hers, eating each and every one of those sexy little noises even as our rhythm increases, her hips lifting slightly to meet every thrust.

Her fingers dig into the small of my back and I relish the feel of her hands all over me. If I could, I would bottle this incredible feeling of rightness. When we're together like this everything makes sense. I reach down and pull one of her legs up and over my hip, trying to get deeper. We both groan at the new angle, the slight change in position making her pussy tighten down like a clamp.

She's moaning my name over and over again and all I can think about is how good it feels when her hands fist in my hair. My mouth latches on to her earlobe and that sends her over, her legs wrapping around my waist like she can't get close enough.

There's no way I can resist the rapid pulses of her body around mine and I let go, riding out the blissful waves of pleasure until we're both left panting and exhausted.

"Holy shit," Anya breathes.

It makes me laugh but it's also exactly what I was thinking. How did we go from talking about everything that happened today to screwing each other's brains out?

As soon as I pull away from her, I'm instantly cold but I also know I probably need to leave. My underwear and slacks are next to my foot but I have to search for a minute before I find my shirt crumpled at the end of the bed. I wince at how several of the buttons are hanging loosely. I button them as best I can. I'm sure the dry cleaners can fix it.

When I look up, Anya is watching me.

"Thank you, Law."

I swipe a hand through my sweaty hair. "You don't have to thank me."

She points at my dick. "Should I thank him?"

Her irreverence smoothes over the awkwardness I'm feeling and as usual, I'm left smiling.

"I should probably go."

Her hand reaches toward me. "Can you stay? For a little while."

Unable to deny her anything, I lie back down.

"I was really scared today," she says finally.

"Your dad is going to be just fine. The doctors said he was lucky, remember?"

"He's fine. Today. But what about tomorrow? Or the day after that? Maybe I've just been in denial but it really hit me tonight that one day he won't be okay." She turns into my embrace and buries her head against my shoulder.

"I'm sorry, baby."

She lets out a long shuddering sigh. "What would he do if my mom wasn't there? When he gets confused, she's always there to pull him back to the here and now. What will I do when I'm his age banging around an apartment by myself?"

The idea of her being older and alone is so foreign and shocking that I go still. Anya continues speaking, so softly I'm not even sure she realizes what she's saying.

"What will my life be like if I don't have a love strong enough to pull me back? Or someone to talk to the doctors for me and make sure that I'm being taken care of?"

"That's not going to be you, Anya." Just the thought of it is painful.

Her fingers dig into my arms. "I know you think marriage is just a piece of paper. But that paper has the power to declare who is family and who isn't."

If she was crying, I could work with that. Tears are my kryptonite but at least I know what they mean.

But it's the quiet certainty in her voice, like she has foreseen her fate and already accepted it, that strikes me through the heart. Because I know in that moment that I want to be a part of her future. I want to be the one holding her hand.

Even if things get hard.

Even if she doesn't remember me.

I'll always want to hold her hand so she'll never feel alone.

For long moments, we stay just like that, her in my arms with my hand tracing a gentle circle on her back. Her breaths are slow and even. When I'm pretty sure she's asleep, I carefully ease back. She wanted me to stay because she was scared and alone but she probably won't be too thrilled to find me here in the morning.

It's the last thing I want to do but I force myself to stand up. After I put my shoes back on, I allow myself the quiet pleasure of watching her sleep for a few minutes before I turn around and tiptoe to the door.

"Law?"

I turn around immediately. "I'm still here, baby."

"Being steady isn't boring. It means that when the chips are down, you're the man who comes through. Every time. It means people can count on you. You give me aspirin in case my head hurts. You remember the dress I left crumpled on the floor. You came to the hospital because my mom needed someone. You're always there."

"I'll always be there for you, Anya. I would do anything for you."

"I know you would," she mumbles sleepily. "If I fell down the stairs because I forgot where they were, you would come and find me."

With a final deep breath, she rolls over to face the wall and I walk out feeling more confused than ever.

———

LUCKILY THAT DAY at work is uneventful. I wait until almost lunchtime to send a text checking on Anya. If she managed to sleep in, then I don't want to wake her. But she responds immediately.

JAMES LAWSON

How are you doing?

ANYA PETROVA

I'm good. Just came over to take my mom back to the hospital. Pop seems better today.

JAMES LAWSON

Let me know if there's anything you need.

She doesn't respond for the rest of the day. I open and close a text to her a hundred times before I decide to give her some space. When I go home that night, I try to distract myself with a movie but by the time I crawl into bed in the early morning hours, the silence is deafening.

Saturday afternoon, I decide to go to the office and get some work done. I used to have a pretty firm rule about never working on weekends but what do I have to stay home for now? So I throw on a pair of sweatpants and a muscle tee before heading out. I'll go to the gym before coming home. It'll be nice to get a decent workout in for once instead of doing some half-assed weightlifting in my garage.

Mya is waiting for the elevator when I walk off.

"James! I didn't think you were coming in today."

"I figured I'd get a few things done. Everything ready for the GlowUp event?"

"All systems go. It should be perfect. I just came in to check a few last minute details. I'm heading over to the theater early to make sure everything is being setup according to my directions. I'll text you updates tonight."

After considering what Anya said about delegating, I'd decided not to attend the event. After how many times I've given him the stink eye, I'm sure Seth Barrington won't be heartbroken that I'm not there.

"Great. I'll see you later."

After about an hour, I realize I'm not getting much done. So I walk two blocks over to the gym near our building and spend a good hour working out. Once I'm sweaty and all my muscles are burning, I finally head home.

After I park in the garage, I enter the house. It takes a minute to register that all the lights are on.

I didn't leave the lights on.

Just when I'm about to go back into the garage and get the hell out of there, Liz turns the corner. She's holding a glass of wine.

All the breath explodes from my lungs. "Nice of you to make yourself at home. How did you get in here?"

Seemingly shocked at my annoyance, she shrugs. "You still keep your key in a potted plant."

"That'll be changing. A lot of things will be changing actually."

She looks amused. "Such as?"

"Don't worry about that. Let's focus on you. I'm guessing Gareth finally got sick of your shit. How long has he been gone?"

The look of shock that flashes over her face is gone just as quickly. Was she always this good at manipulation? Or was I just not looking in the right place?

I throw my gym bag in the corner and get a bottle of Gatorade from the fridge.

"Well? I'm waiting."

Liz huffs. "I don't know what you mean. Gareth is back at home. Where I left him."

"Somehow, I doubt that's the whole story. Let's follow this Yellow Brick Road all the way to the end, shall we? If Gareth bailed, a bunch of your other clients probably jumped ship, too."

Her eyes are hard. "You're reaching. Let me guess. Your little girlfriend convinced you I'm making it up because I'm jealous, right?"

"She didn't have to. It turns out you're as predictable as I am."

What happened is as clear as glass. Liz thought she could show up here and stir the pot the way she always does, planting seeds of doubt right in the middle of my new life.

I chuckle at how easily she almost got away with it. Truthfully, I might not have caught on if I didn't have Anya to call out her bullshit.

That's my girl.

She doesn't lie. She could have just dated billionaire boy and kept me on the side but she was upfront about what she wanted the whole time. Anya has a history of truth and Liz has a history of lies.

"You use people and then when they finally wise up you try to switch targets. This time you miscalculated. You should have picked someone who doesn't know your games."

Liz won't meet my eyes. "I was just trying to apologize to you."

"Apology accepted. But you're still a piece of shit. Now get out or I'm calling the cops."

With one last arctic glare, Liz slams her wineglass on the counter. She snatches her coat off the couch and saunters out, slamming the front door behind her. I watch from the window as she climbs into a car I didn't even notice at the curb.

It's oddly freeing, for the first time in years, not to care what she thinks.

I *am* a creature of habit but Anya made me realize that's

not a bad thing. After hearing her describe me in her adorably sleepy voice, I'll never see myself through Liz's eyes ever again.

Suddenly I need to see her. When I pull out my phone, I see a text message from Mya. Strange for her to text me on a Saturday night. Then I remember that she was going to report back on the GlowUp event.

She's included the GlowUp official launch numbers and various pictures she snapped of the event.

I stop at the last one. It's Seth Barrington.

It's Seth Barrington with Anya on his arm gazing at him adoringly.

My mind races, too stunned to even respond to Mya's last question. Anya is wearing a slinky black dress and hanging on Seth's arm when I assumed that she was at home in bed exhausted or with her parents.

No, she's at a black-tie event looking like my every fucking dream and giving another man that hopeful little smile I used to think was just for me.

My feet move back and forth across the carpet. I can't take my eyes off this picture. She's so beautiful and I know her soul is even more so. Suddenly seeing her is the most important thing in the world.

I need to tell her how I feel.

I need to tell her what I've discovered.

My tuxedo hasn't been pressed but it'll have to do. I jog

back to my room and push to the back of my closet. I have to tell her how I feel before I lose her for good.

Because Anya isn't the only one in that picture with a hopeful smile. Seth Barrington is looking at her with an expression I recognize intimately. It's the same incredulous smile that used to grace my face every morning when I woke up to see Anya's face on the pillow next to mine.

It's the face of a man in love.

## *twenty-two*

ANYA

THE OFFICIAL GLOWUP launch gala is being held at a small community theater called The Starlight. Seth told me it has many art programs he funds for underprivileged youth. Having the gala here will help bring attention to the theater and hopefully encourage some of the attendees to sign up as patrons.

The building is in a less desirable part of the city but I have to admit it's a dramatic scene for a gala. The theater chairs are a deep burgundy velvet and the curtains draping the stage are an inky midnight blue. The ceiling is painted with a mural done by the students.

"Everyone seems like they're having a good time," I whisper to Seth. "Philippe looks like he's having fun."

I was mortified when Seth introduced us earlier. After our closet chat, I never did get around to telling him who the handsome man was who'd once saved me from choking. I have a feeling he'll never let me live that one down.

"Thing are going very well. We exceeded all the estimates. In fact, I was told that the app already has several successful matches reported and even one engagement."

"Seriously? It hasn't even been available that long."

He chuckles. "I guess when you know, you know."

Not to be judgmental but that is just crazy. Then I sigh. I'm probably not the right person to decide what the right length of time is before getting engaged. I thought an engagement was coming just because Law and I had been practically living together and look where that got me.

People wander between the rows of theater seats chatting excitedly. Earlier, the development team and all the investors announced the initial launch numbers to resounding applause.

GlowUp is officially a hit.

As I nod at another person, the smile on my face feels frozen. My hand is tucked in the crook of Seth's elbow so at least I'm not obligated to shake hands or hug. The expectation of a billionaire's date seems to be being glued to his side with a vacant smile on your face.

Or at least that's what most of the women here look like.

Truthfully, I'm kind of grateful not much is expected of me tonight. I am physically and mentally exhausted.

My father is comfortably settled back at home now but

my mother was an emotional wreck when I left today. I wanted to stay but I promised Seth I would be here tonight. Plus, there really isn't anything else I can do for her. The guilt of my father getting hurt is a burden she seems determined to bear. The thought that he might not be able to live at home for much longer weighs on me heavily.

Why does it feel like everything is falling apart?

"After they announce the app is officially live to the public we can leave," Seth murmurs before lifting his hand in a wave to someone across the room. "I'm sure this is the last place you want to be right now."

"I'm sorry I'm such a bummer."

He squeezes my arm. "You don't have to apologize. How is your dad doing?"

"He's better. His wrist was sprained and not broken so that was good. I'm honestly more worried about my mom. She blames herself for not hearing him leave the apartment."

"That's tough. I can't imagine how hard that must be for her."

"I can't either. At least she finally agreed to get a security system. Now it sounds an alarm when the door is opened."

"Good. What about you?"

"Me? I'm fine."

"Are you?" His eyes are probing.

"I will be. What about you? How are things with your shady friend?" I feel bad that we spend so much time talking about my drama.

Now that we've moved away from the stage, it's a little easier to talk. Even though people's eyes follow Seth wherever he goes, being on the outskirts of the crowd makes it look like we're having an intimate little moment. No one approaches.

I guess even billionaires don't want to cock-block each other.

He snorts out a laugh. "Well, you called it. You were right about him."

Shocked, I lean back so I can see his face. "I was? You mean shady guy really was shady?"

"I asked my accountant to do some checking on our projects. There are definitely some things that don't add up. Now he's suddenly not returning my calls."

"I wish I'd been wrong. I wanted to be."

"It's okay. I don't need friends. I have a brother. That's bad enough."

In spite of everything, he makes me smile.

"You have friends. I'm your friend. Maybe we're not meant to be but at the very least, we are friends. You can't get rid of me now."

"We *have* bonded," he concedes. "I bought you cock. You owe me for life now."

He says this just as a waiter approaches. The young man's eyes almost bug out of his head. Then he turns bright red.

"More champagne?" he squeaks.

Seth places his empty glass on the waiter's tray and takes another. My shoulders shaking, I accept the glass he hands me.

After the waiter hurries away I say, "Well, we just traumatized him. No matter how bad things get, there will always be something to laugh at."

He raises his glass. "To laughter."

———

WE'VE DONE another circuit of the room and Seth is getting ready for the final announcement when we hear sudden loud voices. I look around trying to find the source. Several other people are doing the same thing. Whatever is going on must be outside the theater.

A big burly guy suddenly appears at Seth's elbow.

"What's going on, Eddie?" Seth asks.

"There's been some kind of breach. Sir, we need to get you out of here until–"

Just then someone bursts into the theater. A woman screams as the door knocks her backward. People start running for the other exit.

Eddie and some other huge guy who appears out of nowhere are suddenly standing between us and the door.

"*Anya!* Where are you?"

The sound of my name makes me peek my head around the big guy in front of me. Law is standing in the middle of the aisle, looking around the room frantically. He's dressed in a tux but it looks like he found it in the bottom of a trash can and his hair is standing on end. There is something dark smeared on his right cheek.

Basically, he looks terrible.

"Oh my god. *Law?*"

The big guys move forward at once and I realize they're going to grab him. Seth suddenly moves around them holding his arms up.

"He's with me, guys. It's okay."

The security personnel who came from the back of the theater glance over at Law skeptically.

"Sir, are you sure?"

While Seth handles the security, I walk down the aisle toward Law. Now that he's no longer being pursued, he collapses into the closest theater seat.

"Law, what are you doing? And why do you look..."

At a complete loss for words, I gesture up and down his body, just now noticing that he's also missing a shoe.

"I forgot my wallet and those goons at the front wouldn't believe me when I told them I was on the list!"

Seth had mentioned the security would be tight. Any event he's publicized to attend requires heightened security. Now I'm starting to understand why.

Obviously Law doesn't mean him any harm but if he got in here, someone who was dangerous probably could as well.

"That's not what I meant. I am kind of curious how you got around security but I meant why are you *here*? You could have just texted me later."

"No, I couldn't. I had to come before it was too late."

Suddenly I'm aware of a strong fishy odor. My hand covers my nose.

What is that?

I look around searching for the source and notice there is a hole in the toe of Law's sock. Did he step in something gross?

"Too late for what?"

He shakes his head. "I had it all wrong. Marriage didn't make Liz a different person. She was always that way I was just too dumb to see it. Labels don't make someone shitty."

"I'm glad you realize that, Law. But what does that have to do with me? We want different things. I want different things."

"You want love." He stands and walks toward me. When he's close enough, he reaches out and takes my hand. "*I love you.*"

My throat is so thick with tears I can barely breathe. This is the first time he's ever said the words and the impact reverberates through my entire body. I try to pull my hand back but he holds tight.

"Don't say that. It's not fair to say things you don't mean just because I'm moving on."

"That's not why I'm saying it. The last woman I gave those words to threw them back in my face along with my ring and my trust. I actually thought if I didn't say them, I wouldn't feel that way again."

The people around us have fallen back giving us space. The music has stopped. If you'd asked me how I thought this day would end, I never could have predicted this. This is the craziest thing I've ever seen Law do. I can't believe Mr. Straight and Narrow is making a scene.

For me.

Oblivious to everyone staring, Law pulls me closer.

"*I love you.* I have for a long time. That doesn't change because you slap a label on it. Pretending not to be your boyfriend didn't change my feelings. Calling you my wife won't make our love disappear."

Even though I don't want it to my heart flips hearing him say the word *wife*. Just as quickly I tell her to take a seat.

"I don't want you to marry me just to keep me happy. I

refuse to be one of those women dragging a guy to the altar in chains."

He laughs. "I'm not asking yet. I'd prefer not to smell like sewer water when I do."

"Oh my god, is that smell coming from you?"

"Don't ask. You don't want to know what I landed in the first time they threw me out."

Seth walks down the aisle just then. "Sorry to interrupt. Is everything okay?"

Law glowers at him but I move between them. After escaping security the last thing he needs is to start something with Seth.

"Everything is fine."

He nods. "I take it that means I'm on my own for the rest of the night."

"It does. Sorry."

"Don't be. Good luck."

After he walks away, I hold out my hand to Law. "Let's go home."

His shoulders sag. "Thank God. Not trying to be dramatic but there's something moving in my sock. And I really want to kiss you but I can't while I stink like this."

"Don't worry. It'll keep."

# twenty-three

LAW

"I DON'T THINK I've ever appreciated a shower more."

From her perch on the bed, Anya laughs. "After riding all the way home with that smell, I would have to agree."

I sit on the edge of the bed. My ruined tuxedo is crumpled in the corner. That'll have to go to the incinerator. I'll never be able to wear it again without a flashback of being tossed into the street.

Anya shifts so she can see my face. "So what happened tonight before you showed up at the event?"

"Liz happened."

Her smile tightens. "I should have known she wouldn't go quietly into the night."

"I'm glad she didn't. It was good to finally tell her that I don't give a shit what she thinks anymore. She tried all her usual tricks, calling me predictable and boring. I just didn't care."

"What changed? Don't get me wrong, I'm happy. I actually would pay money to have seen her face when you told her to hit the road. I guess I'm just wondering what's different now?"

She picks at the edge of the blanket, the vulnerable expression on her face twisting my heart into knots. Her eyes telegraph her thoughts like a bullhorn.

*Why should I believe you've changed?*

*How do I know you won't break my heart again?*

"I don't have her voice in my head anymore. Now it's *you*. You telling me that I'm steadfast and strong and someone you depend on. Liz always wanted more, like I would never be enough. But you, the only thing you ever wanted was me."

"That's still all I want."

"I've let you down in so many ways but one day, I'll earn your love again."

She leans her head against my arm. "You never lost it. I will love you until the day I die."

My stomach rumbles and we both laugh.

"This is terrible timing but I'm really hungry."

She scrambles off the bed and grabs my hands. "Um, this is me you're talking to. It's never a bad time for food."

I follow her to the kitchen and open the fridge. We have

stuff for sandwiches and some leftover frozen pizza. I pull out the sandwich fixings while Anya opens the pantry. When she comes back she has a package of Oreos and a bag of cheese pretzels.

"It's been a long night. I'm eating everything."

"Trust me. I'm not judging."

My phone dings with a text message. I pull it out of my pocket and see it's a new message from Mya. I'm almost afraid to open it.

It's finally sinking in that I just made a flaming fool of myself in front of several employees and quite a few clients.

But I have to check it. She might have a legitimate issue with the event.

After reading it, I put the phone down. "Mya got the cabaret account."

Anya grins. "Of course she did. That woman is a badass."

"Hell yeah, she is. She invited them to the GlowUp gala. According to her, their CEO reported this as the most exciting event he's been to in ages."

"It's not every day a wild man comes running in missing a shoe."

Laughing, we bundle everything on a tray and take our little snack back to the bedroom. We eat in companionable silence then I put the tray on the dresser. After I turn out the lights, Anya slips under the covers. I climb in next to her and rest my head on the pillow.

She sighs.

I sigh.

"This is what I've been missing."

She chuckles. "Late night snack attacks?"

"You. Being here. This is all I want in the world."

She snuggles closer and I rest my head on top of hers.

"Anya," I whisper.

"Yes," she whispers back.

"When I ask you it won't be just because you want it. I'll be asking because I can't stand the thought of you not being mine."

# twenty-four

ANYA

"I OFFICIALLY CALL this Girl's Night to order!"

Mya grabs Ari's arm and pulls her down on the couch. "Will you sit down and hush so Anya can give us the scoop."

We're all gathered here in Ariana's apartment on a Monday evening, drinking margaritas that Casey made. Jessi already knows what happened but I figured I'd better get the rest of the girls together so I'd only have to tell the whole crazy story one more time.

"You cannot keep us in suspense. The entire office is buzzing about James running into the event looking like he got mugged or something. What the hell happened?" Mya asks.

I snickered. Today at work was more than a little awkward. Poor Law spent most of the day hiding in his office. Whenever anyone asked me about the event I just shrugged.

Let them wonder.

"Law got an unexpected visit from his ex-wife. She's been sniffing around since last week."

"Who is she? Do we need to find this bitch?" Ariana pushes her sleeves up.

Mya sighs. "Calm down, Rocky. I'm sure she flew back to California on her broom by now."

"Hopefully. But it was enough for Law to realize he's been letting his baggage with her ruin our relationship. He said he wanted to catch me at the event before it was too late. Although I'm not sure how he knew I was there with Seth."

Mya tentatively raises her hand. "I might have had something to do with that."

"Well, I'm grateful. We talked and things are good now. He's been good. After years of hearing his ex telling him he was boring and not good enough, now he knows that's not true. He's exactly what I want."

"I get how he felt," Ariana says.

Mya looks at her, shocked. "You understand? Mistress Bitterness can sympathize with emotions?"

"What?" Ari says defensively. "I can be emotional. Sometimes. After watching my parents fight I didn't think a relationship was in the cards for me. Or friends. I used to do weird stuff thinking it would keep people away from me."

"Like carrying a demon baby doll on the subway?" Mya comments.

"Or wearing a snorkel and wetsuit the first time we met?" Casey chimes in.

Ariana shrugs. "That was easier than being disappointed all the time. But it turns out letting my inner weirdo out didn't just drive the wrong people away, it attracted the right people. It got me you guys, didn't it?"

"Awww. Ari, that's actually really sweet!" Casey leans over for a hug. Mya wraps her arms around them both. Unable to resist, I join in, resting my head on Mya's shoulder.

Ariana yells, "Too much estrogen in the room!"

After that, conversation turns to Mya's upcoming visit back to her parents' hometown in Barbados and whether we should plan an island getaway for a Girl's Night trip. Once the margaritas are all gone, Ariana takes the pitcher into the kitchen. I follow carrying our glasses.

"Did you ever think our pact would lead us here."

She laughs. "Our pact got us both what we wanted in the end."

"Does this mean you're finally going to introduce me to your guy?"

"Yes. We'll have you guys over for dinner really soon.

It's finally time. Actually, there's something else I've been meaning to tell you. Now that you're all *happily-ever-aftered* I don't have to worry that it'll be too deep."

She takes a deep breath and then starts singing.

*Check One. Check Two.*

*I want to share some news with you!*

After waving her arms around, she ends with a hip thrust.

Mya is just entering the room when Ari starts moving. She starts shaking her head and waving her arms.

"Oh no. Ari, what did we talk about? *This is not how you tell people serious news!*"

She drags Ari out of the room by the arm. We can hear them fussing all the way into the hallway.

Then Ari whines, "*But I changed the dance moves!*"

I look over at Casey. "What was that?"

She shakes her head. "That's a whole other story. Trust me. You'll need to get comfortable for this one."

# *epilogue*

## ANYA

I STEP out onto the balcony and raise my face into the breeze. After being in the crush of people, the crisp air feels fantastic. Tonight is my parents' thirtieth wedding anniversary and we are celebrating with all of their friends and even some extended family that came to visit from Russia.

It's been a rough year but a beautiful one, too. We found a fantastic nurse for Pop. Now my mom has some help and has been able to keep him home longer. I'm under no illusions that this will last forever, but whatever comes next, we'll handle it together. The way we always do.

A hand wraps around my waist and I melt back into the embrace. Law's lips are warm against my chilled skin when he kisses my neck.

"Your dad just beat me at cards again." His lips curl against my skin. "He seemed shocked at how bad I still am."

"Who were you today?" I ask.

"Arty. Your mom said Artyom was his best friend at university. High praise, apparently."

"It is. According to some of the stories I've heard, those two did everything together. Although I'm sure he would have never told those stories if he'd known I was listening."

His arm tightens around my waist. "I wish I'd known him before."

I turn around to face him. His vulnerability is touching. Over the last year he has come so far from the man who was afraid to trust or to love.

Now his heart is wide open and I can feel his regret at the time we lost. Because if things had been different, maybe he could have spent time with my father before his condition deteriorated so much.

"Me too. He would have loved you. But I think on some level he knows you even now."

"Really? Even though I'm someone different every time?"

"Have you noticed that even though the name changes, it's always someone he loved?"

A tender smile crosses his lips. "I hadn't thought of it that way. I'm honored. I hope somewhere deep down he approves of me for his daughter."

"I think my mother approves enough for the both of them. She is your biggest fan. After yours truly, of course."

I look over my shoulder. Through the glass I can see into the living room where my mom has been perched next to Pop all night. The only time she has left his side was for food. She is a living example of the excellent advice she gave me to cherish every moment.

Law's phone dings and he pulls it out. Then he whistles softly. "Whoa. You are not going to believe this. I have the Lady Whistledown scoop of the *season*."

I crack up. After convincing him to join me on my third Netflix binge of the Bridgerton series, he is now just as obsessed with the show as I am.

Even if he tries to *pretend* he hates it.

"What happened?"

He angles his phone so I can see the screen. I was expecting a trending topic on social media or a news headline. But it's an email message from one of his friends.

"Sunfire filed for bankruptcy?"

He shakes his head. "I heard some whispers a few months ago that not only did she lose a bunch of clients when Gareth left, but that others had complained of being overcharged."

I'm trying so hard to play surprised but I've never had much of a poker face.

Law narrows his eyes. "You already knew?"

I wince. "Maybe?"

He crosses his arms. "Spill."

"Okay, you know how Liz claimed her employee was getting information from me. She wasn't exactly wrong. Except for one little detail. I barely talked to Donna except for when she'd email asking for advice about how to bill clients."

He covers his mouth with his hand but I can see that he's smiling. "What did you do?"

"Nothing! She was charging clients the wrong amounts and putting way too few manhours on the estimates. I just didn't correct her. I wasn't going to do her job for her."

"So that's why they were underbidding us. And eventually they underbid so much that they couldn't afford to do the work for those prices."

I shrug. "No idea. It's none of my business."

He pulls me into a kiss. "Diabolical woman. I love the way your wicked little mind works."

The sound of music from inside the apartment catches both of our attention. My parents are dancing to their wedding song while all the guests watch. Law pulls me into his arms and we sway together to the muted strains of the music.

"Do you ever want more for us?"

Lulled by the sound of the music and his warm arms, I hum an agreement.

"Like this?" He inclines his head toward the party.

I follow his eyes to where my mom and dad are dancing. What he's getting at finally dawns on me.

"You don't like weddings," I whisper.

"I like what they represent. I don't care if you're wearing a big white dress. All I want is the two of us making promises. Making plans. Sharing—"

"Everything," I finish for him as I read the unasked question in his eyes.

For a moment we stand frozen, our hearts beating together as the entirety of our future, all the possibilities, hangs there between us. His eyes ask, and my eyes answer, before his head dips for a kiss.

"Everything," he says and just before his lips cover mine he whispers, "including a last name."

———

I hope you enjoyed *Want Me.*

**Want More?** When you join my VIP list, *The Minions,* you get access to a FREE bonus vault filled with goodies, (both ebooks & audiobooks). So come join us at mmalonebooks.com/newsletter

———

Are you a fan of small town gossip and grumpy heroes? If so, you'll love *You Ruin Everything*! It's pure romantic comedy with a zany family, a pug with a vendetta and a heroine you can root for!

HE'S grumpy and shirtless and good with his hands. But he's also my best friend's brother and the bane of my existence! Surely we can be roommates for one summer without burning the house down, right? **Start reading now!**

—————

The wedding shenanigans continue! Up next is Ariana's book, *Need Me*. You won't believe all the drama that goes down during the reception. Everyone's favorite crazy roomie finally meets her match. Her story crosses timelines with this book so you'll get to see the other side of the Anya-Ariana pact! **Get NEED ME now!**

Although I have to warn you, this book is best avoided if you are in any danger of peeing when you laugh. You'll understand when you get to the grocery store scene. Or the BBQ scene. Just… trust me.

**A hilarious twist on *How to Lose a Guy in Ten Days* about the last single woman in her friend group who meets "Mr. Right" at the "wrong" time.**

Happily Ever After is overrated. There I said it. Call me a buzzkill but after watching all of my friends and roommates succumb to the love virus, I've decided to sit this one out. I've made a game of seeing how far I can push before guys go running. Until I meet my match. He makes me laugh. He listens. And all the crazy stuff I do doesn't even faze him. Which is a problem when I find out he has the power to ruin my best friend's career.

So I'm taking the gloves off. It's time for Operation: Get

Rid of Mr. Perfect. If being crazy didn't get rid of him maybe I have to try the scariest thing of all. Being myself.

*NEED ME is a "How to Lose a Guy in Ten Days" type of romantic comedy. Get ready to laugh in inappropriate places! This* **standalone** *romance features crossover characters from the USA TODAY bestselling book BEG ME.*

Get NEED ME now!
at minxmalone.com/needme

Excerpt of *NEED ME* © 2020 M. Malone

## VIN

I scowl down at the bowl of soup and the sleeve of crackers on the tray. If I never have to look at another bowl of soup or porridge again I'll be content.

Getting hit by a car was no picnic but I'm not dying. This food is making me feel like I have one foot in the grave already.

That's it. I'm going out. They told me that I should take it easy for a few days. They didn't say anything about treating me like a grandfather or boring me to death.

"Where are you going? You're supposed to be resting." Andre asks in Italian, gesturing to the bed.

We usually speak Italian when we're alone since he's not concerned about practicing his English. The Italian accent simply adds to his mystique and of course, women love it. Funny how the same people who admire the accent in social situations assume it means you're less competent in business negotiations.

I sigh. "I'm just going for a walk. I need to stretch my legs."

"I'll come with you."

"No!"

He looks a little hurt so I run a hand through my hair. It's not my brother's fault that his presence inevitably draws a crowd. But I can't deal with that today.

"You have a lot to do getting ready for the marketing launch. You don't need to babysit me. I'm just going to stretch my legs. Maybe find us some snacks. I'm sure there must be a shop or grocery close by."

He looks dubious at the idea. Probably just the idea of buying your own groceries is what's throwing him off. We are definitely spoiled by the lifestyle we grew up living.

"Okay, just be careful. Do you have your phone?"

"Yes, *Mamma*. Don't worry so. I'm a big boy now."

He scowls. "I would have thought so but then you walked in front of a taxi."

"Sorry about that. Especially since I pulled you away from the beautiful Mya."

"That wasn't going to happen anyway. But going to the agency for marketing meetings should be interesting going forward."

"You just had to hit on a woman working on the most important launch of our company's history?"

He's already walking away but he gives me the finger over his shoulder. I'm still chuckling by the time I change into a pair of jeans and a cashmere sweater from last year's line. It fits perfectly and is long enough to cover the bandages on my sprained wrist. I need to get out of here before Andre notices I'm wearing something that's out of season.

Once I'm out of the hotel, I use my phone to search out the closest grocery. Then I use the navigation to point me toward a place called Trader Joe's. Whenever we plan to spend extended time in a city, I always investigate the best clubs and restaurants but I've never really thought about things like groceries before. Living out of a hotel means you don't have to.

But today, I want to feel normal. I need to be around people and noise and life. As I walk the chatter of the people I pass flows around me. The many different American accents are a fascinating jumble and then there are the occasional foreign accents thrown in. Being the capital, DC always maintains a healthy community of dignitaries and visitors from other countries along with many foreign exchange students. Although I know it's not Andre's favorite place, I always love it when we come here.

The entrance to the store is covered in a riot of flowers. The blooms are festive and my mood lifts instantly. Shoppers mill around outside looking at the potted plants and there are even bales of hay strewn around the displays. Before I came to America for the first time I'd imagined meeting cowboys on every corner. The reality wasn't quite as fun but I can admit to still carrying a bit of fascination for the idea even now.

Following the crowd, I take a little basket just like the woman in front of me. It shouldn't be that difficult to blend in. I'll just watch what everyone else does and then follow suit. There are large displays of vegetables set around the open space. It reminds me of the outdoor markets in Europe. The woman I'm following picks up some kind of melon and taps it.

Is that how you're supposed to choose fruit? I pick up a clump of bananas and tap them before placing them in my basket. This grocery thing isn't so bad. Next I see a display of large tomatoes. I tap several before choosing one that looks the biggest. A man in the aisle next to me stares as I pick up an orange and tap it.

Am I doing it wrong?

When I turn to observe how everyone else is picking fruits, I bump into the person behind me.

"Sorry, sir. I didn't see you."

The sweet voice doesn't match the devilish face that comes into view when I turn.

"Oh my god. You have got to be kidding me." Ariana waves the cucumber in her hand at me. "How does this keep happening?"

"I told you already. Fate."

———

## *ARIANA*

What is it with this guy? First in the bar, then in the hospital and now I can't even manhandle phallic-shaped veggies without him hanging over my shoulder.

He calls it fate. But it's probably more like karma. The universe seems to be having a good laugh shoving the one guy I might actually want in my face at the exact time in my life that I can't keep him.

That thought reminds me of the appointment I have coming up that I've been ignoring. With a sigh, I place the cucumber I've been waving around in my basket before moving on to the peppers.

"I hope you're making something that tastes better than the bland shit I've been eating lately."

He peers into my basket curiously before I can switch it

to the other arm. His wrist still has a splint on it but his long sleeves cover most of it. He looks a little odd wearing a cashmere sweater when it's so hot outside and his hair definitely hasn't seen a brush in days but otherwise he looks like a slightly rumpled guy with a perfectly stubbled jaw.

I blow out a breath. The man really is too sexy for his own good. Which means I need to get rid of him. Stat.

"Is this a good orange?" He holds it up and taps the side, putting his ear next to the peel.

"What are you doing?"

"Tapping it. Isn't that how you do it? I saw a woman tapping her fruit so I thought it was supposed to sound a certain way."

Holding back a smile, I take the orange from his hand and place it in his basket. "You only tap certain fruits. Usually melons."

He looks disappointed. "Oh. And I was enjoying it so much."

As I move to the salad section, I'm acutely aware of him following closely. This can't really be a coincidence, can it? Seeing him in this many places in DC has to violate all the laws of statistics. But I can't deny the little flash of pleasure that zipped through me when I saw him. He has a way of grinning that makes me feel it all the way down to my toes. Like seeing me has made his day.

It's the kind of thing that's really hard to forget.

When he reaches in the next display case for a single serving of salad, his sleeve moves back revealing the splint. I tell myself that I'm just checking him out in a medical sense, making sure he's really okay after his accident. When he catches me watching him, his lips curl.

"Keeping a close eye on me, *bella*?"

"I'm just looking at your wrist. You seem to be healing nicely. That's good."

His brow furrows. "That's it? You aren't going to ask how I felt about you abandoning me at the hospital?"

"I didn't abandon you. My shift was over and I had to go."

"Uh huh. Well, I was very hurt. First you fall asleep on me. Then you abandon me."

"I didn't–"

He continues, clearly on a roll now that I can't escape. "Your continued indifference to my feelings is very hard on me. Almost as hard as wanking with a sprained wrist. That was a real challenge. Thank you for asking."

"I wasn't going to ask. I figured you'd manage somehow."

He shrugs. "Being ambidextrous had to come in handy at some point."

Not wanting him to see my smile, I move away from the produce and suddenly notice all the people who *definitely* just heard what he said.

An older lady with her almost white hair styled in a profusion of rigid curls watches us with an open mouth. My face heats.

For the first time in years, I'm feeling something. It's unfamiliar but I think it might be… embarrassment?

He's done the impossible. He's managed to out-crazy me.

Get NEED ME now!

at minxmalone.com/needme

### *BEATRICE*

Thinking about trying a dating app? My advice- *don't.* Seriously, save yourself.

If I wasn't on a dating app, I never would have been hiding in the bathroom of an Italian restaurant to avoid the most aggressive of Crypto Bros. And I never would have called the one person who *always* bails me out. August Gordon.

Once upon a time he was the adorkable guy who helped me with my biology homework. Now he is six-foot one with eyes like a dream. Now he's the guy who kissed me on the forehead before saying something that made Crypto Bro look scared for his life.

Nope. This is not happening.

I am not falling for my best friend. Because things between us have always been easy. Uncomplicated.

But if there's one thing I'm good at, it's complicating things.





**BEATRICE**

I can't let him come outside with me. I already told him I called an Uber so I don't want him to see Auggie waiting for me.

And I *definitely* don't want Auggie to see him.

It's not like we haven't talked about dating before but something about Auggie actually seeing me on a date feels weird. Luca seemed good-looking on his profile, but standing next to August, I'm pretty sure he'll look like a pale imitation of what a man should be.

Actually seeing Auggie is pretty much a guarantee to kill any date, even if the guy isn't glued to his phone.

"You should go ahead," I continue. "It was nice meeting you, Luca."

But his grip only tightens, his voice holding a trace of annoyance as he says, "You're not going to let me see you home, Bea? You already spent half the time in the bathroom and now you're leaving early? That's just rude."

I pull back, trying to yank my arm free. "What?"

His aggression is startling, an unwelcome shift from the apathetic facade he displayed earlier. I figured he'd be a little disappointed but not this upset. Then again, nothing about this date has been what I imagined it would be.

"You're one of those women who just use men. You just wanted a free dinner and now you're trying to ditch me," he snaps.

His words echo in my head. Yes, I was trying to ditch him, but not for the reasons he thought.

"Um, I paid for my half of dinner. So..."

I wasn't going to message him again anyway but after this sudden show of aggression, I no longer feel even slightly bad about that decision. Now I just need to get away. But before I can respond, or turn to walk away, I see a familiar figure come through the door of the restaurant.

August.

He takes in my stance next to the booth and Luca's hand on my arm with a darkening scowl. Luca follows my gaze to see what I'm looking at and he glances at me uncertainly as August heads our way.

"You're going to want to let go of her arm now," Auggie growls.

"Who are you?" Luca asks.

Instead of answering, Auggie steps closer until he's right up in Luca's face. The move breaks his hold on my arm, thankfully and I rub the spot which is already getting sore. Auggie sweeps his arm around, folding me close against his back and out of Luca's sight.

"Don't look at her," Auggie barks when Luca tries to look around him at me. "Talk to me."

"I don't even know you," Luca mutters.

"Exactly. And you don't know her either. From this moment on, you have permanent amnesia when it comes to her. Got it?"

"Wait a minute. You can't just–"

Auggie turns around, completely ignoring my blustering date behind him. His lips against my forehead shock me out of the trance I've been in since he showed up.

"Go wait for me right outside, okay?" Auggie says in a low voice.

"Okay," I mumble, not entirely sure what's going on but happy to get away.

Auggie watches me as I walk to the door of the restaurant. Once I push through, he turns back to Luca. There is a large party coming in at the same time as I'm leaving so I step aside to let them through. Once it's clear, I step back up to the window to look back in. The guys are still talking but all I can see are their profiles. Auggie seems to tower over Luca, and with every word the other man seems to shrink. As Auggie continues to speak, Luca's shoulders hunch, his earlier bravado crumbling under August's intensity.

Finally August steps away and when he turns, his face is completely blank. Our eyes meet through the window and the air buzzes with something electric. Caught, I quickly step back and stare aimlessly at the cars going by. My heart is racing for some reason I can't identify.

What was that? I wouldn't have believed it if I hadn't seen it myself. My aggressive date had been completely shut down by whatever Auggie said.

And I am completely turned on.


Join the fun at patreon.com/minxmalone

**Ask Me** : Am I arrogant? Maybe. Do women still want me? Abso-F'ing-lutely. Then I meet the one woman who isn't impressed.

**Want Me** : No strings attached. Sounds good, right? Except if I'm not her boyfriend ... the position is open for someone else.

**Need Me** : Crazy sh*t every day keeps relationships away. Except there's one guy who just *keeps* showing up. And if I'm not careful, I might get used to needing someone.

## BLUE-COLLAR BILLIONAIRES

*Inheriting billions from the father they never knew sounds like a pretty sweet deal. Until they find out what he really wants in exchange.*

**Tank** : Fake Dating the billionaire's son should have been easy. He's a bad boy and not my type. But he's also loyal and kind with an unexpected soft spot for rescue cats. Suddenly all I want is for this "fake" love to be real.

**Finn** : When she left me, I had nothing. Now I have it all: money, cars and most importantly, power. She's struggling to save her business, and I'm in the perfect position to save it. For a price.

**Gabe** : She thinks I'm arrogant and cocky as hell. She's right. A reformed con artist and a perfect little princess don't belong together. But I still can't leave her alone.

**Zack** : She's my brother's ex. Off limits. But she needs a nude model for her show so I'm taking one for the team. Turns out she needs more than just my picture...

**Luke** : My online BFF is the only hacker better than I am. Then

I'm asked to consult on a hacking case for the FBI and the hauntingly beautiful suspect seems to know a lot about me. Things I've only told one other person...

**Blue-Collar Christmas** : Emma has a plan to bring the high-rolling billionaire Marshall brothers back to their roots with the perfect blue-collar Christmas. But it turns out the "perfect" Christmas has a price tag no one expected...

# BAD BUSINESS

## (The Kingsleys)

**Bad King**: My parents just put a gold diggers target on my back. But if all they want is a wedding, I'll find the fiancee of their nightmares. *Who Wants to Marry a Billionaire? Must be completely inappropriate.*

**Bad Blood** : I'd do anything for my best friend's little sister. Until she asks for the one thing I can't give. One night. No rules. ***RITA® Award Winner!***

# THE ALEXANDERS

**One More Day** : "Good girl" Ridley has always attracted bad guys. Now she's on the run and has nowhere to hide. So when Jackson Alexander mistakes her for her twin, she decides to do something she knows is wrong. *She lies.*

**The Things I Do for You** : Nick Alexander finally has what

the woman of his dreams needs. He'll give Raina a baby if she gives
him what he wants. *Her.*

**All I Want**: All Kaylee wants is for Elliott Alexander to notice
she's alive. When her car skids out of control on Christmas Eve,
she's forced to reach out to the only man she trusts to save her.
**(VIP List only)**

**All I Need is You** : When the man she loves leaves town after
their steamy kiss, Kaylee Wilhelm is done. But when she's targeted
by a stalker, Eli is the only one who can protect her.

**Just One Thing** : Bennett Alexander is a bona fide genius but he
still can't figure out how to "get the girl". So he hires a dating tutor.
What could go wrong? Other than falling for his teacher, of course.

**One More Chance** : Now that Ridley is expecting, everything
is different. All she needs is for Jackson to pretend that he finds her
as sexy as he used to, even if it's not true. But with a little advice
from her meddlesome twin, she has a plan to seduce her own
husband.

## THE SIMMONS

**Birthday Cake** : Ever since Mara walked into her brother's
dorm room freshman year and came face to face with a shirtless
Trent, she's known he was *The One*. She finally has a plan to get
him exactly where she wants him. *In her bed.*

**He's the Man** : Matt Simmons is over Army doctors poking him
until he sees his old babysitter, now a physical therapist, is h-o-t.
Suddenly he's seeing the benefits of therapy.

**Say You Will** : Mara Simmons has always known Trent Townsend is *The One*. But when she suspects his frequent business trips have *nothing* to do with business, she sets in motion a chain of events bigger than she can imagine and discovers that the man she loves just might be a stranger.

**Join my VIP list for FREE books**

**newsletter.mmalonebooks.com**

## *about the author*

M. Malone is a RITA® Award winner and a NYT & USA Today Bestselling author of completely inappropriate romantic comedy. She lives with her husband and their two sons in the picturesque mountains of Northern Virginia even though she is afraid of insects, birds, butterflies and other humans.

She also holds a Master's degree in Business from a prestigious college that would no doubt be scandalized at how she's using her expensive education.

**mmalonebooks.com**

9 781938 789700